Vicky!

Thank you &
Enjoy my dark sid

Jack Ladd
x

CW00729589

1

OSCAR

JACK LADD

To know light, you must first know the dark.

WARNING
This book contains sexually explicit content only suitable for mature readers.

Preface

Initially published online, the first chapter of *Oscar* was written one cold, wet Wednesday afternoon in late 2015.

It began as an exercise. A writing workout to stop my brain from frying at my keyboard after I'd come to a road block in my first novel, *Oscar Down Under: Part One* (the first in a series of tales based on my life-changing years spent living, learning and loving in Sydney, Australia).

However, as the weeks progressed, and my writer's block vanished, I realised there was more to Oscar than his life Down Under, and that if I wanted to do him any justice, I would need to start at the beginning.

It was then I knew that *Oscar* wasn't just an exercise. It was a prequel. The first in a series of prequel novels leading up to his journey to the other side of the world and a dark, extremely graphic articulation of the sexualised generation he belongs to.

This book is an edited and remastered version of the story that was published online in full, chapter by chapter each fortnight, from late 2015 to early 2017.

Warning, this story isn't for the faint-hearted.

One

I was the first gay kid at my school.

The first people knew about.

Where I'm from, word gets around quick. People talk: it's human nature. When someone in my class caught me leaving a bowling alley toilet cubicle with another teenage boy on a Sunday evening, red-faced and with a bulge down my jean leg, even if we'd only been snorting coke the rumours would have spread like wildfire.

And boy did they burn.

Luckily for the other kid, he went to a different school. A posh, private school with tuition running into the tens of thousands of pounds per term. Less than a mile from the gates of mine, but so socially and economically distant, he may as well have been royalty. Cut off from the peasants.

Cut off, hidden and protected.

Unluckily for me, we hadn't been snorting coke. And, while I hadn't had a choice in what happened next, if I could, I wouldn't have changed it for the world.

It made me who I am today.

It wasn't the easiest: understatement of the fucking century. Especially at an all-boys grammar school. Free education served on a plate of high expectations and expected gratitude, surrounded by a steaming, undulating throng of testosterone.

But, school had been fine up until that Sunday evening. Not good but not bad. I'd never been much at making friends, so I'd kept to myself. Stuck to the shadows. Stayed out of trouble.

I'd known I was different since I'd figured out how to wank. I'd tried, beating off to pictures of girls on the Internet. Grainy videos of desperation that proved one thing and one thing only.

Look at the boys.

And I had. I'd looked and thought about them plenty. Talked to plenty whenever I'd had a chance. Watched them in the classroom and on the field. Outside of school and on the bus home.

I'd relished it. Knowing I was different. Silently enjoying the spoils from the background. Until I hadn't been able stay in the background anymore. Until my body had yearned for more than stolen glances on rickety, old coaches and blissful but agonisingly brief brushes of skin against skin in noisy corridors.

Until I'd discovered Gaydar and my world had expanded like a supernova. Until I'd finally been able to talk to other people like me. Learn from them. Meet up with them.

Get caught.

When I walked in the next day, the Monday after, naturally there were problems. The kid who'd seen us didn't hold back. He told everyone.

First came name calling. Then segregation. Then violence.

But even though it hurt, and the rage of revenge simmered and boiled for years after, there was another feeling. A feeling I hadn't expected.

Relief.

Even when a gang circled me in the quad at break, and did what they did to me, a part of me didn't care.

I'm free.

Free from normality. Free from pretending to be the person everyone else had wanted me to be. Free from the mundane crap fed to me on TV and in movies and by society.

Grow up. Have kids. Work like a dog to buy a house. Keep working until its paid off. Slowly get old and fade into nothing.

The same shit on repeat every day until I die.

And, like the juiciest cherry on top of the whole sweet and sour situation, I soon found out there were other perks to being the first openly gay guy at my school.

I wasn't shocked when my MSN messenger started bleeping with friend requests from lads that had never spoken to me in their lives.

Naturally they didn't dare speak to me in person. And I didn't blame them after what had happened to me. But behind the anonymity of a keyboard they unloaded all sorts. All kinds of hormone-enriched desires and fantasies.

It was like I'd suddenly become the only flame in a world full of adolescent moths, and life was getting hotter by the days.

My favourite came a month after I'd recovered from the incident in the quad. Three weeks back to school.

Adam Stanmore.

Adam, was special. Not because we fell in love, oh no. Our story's not one of sunshine and lollipops. It was what he represented.

Adam was the leader. The head of the pack and King of School. Six-foot-six, he was the guy every boy wanted to be and every girl wanted to be with. He was captain of the rugby team and his house parties were legendary.

I was a social outcast that no team wanted, who had turned to the solitude of swimming and jogging to keep the Gaydar messages coming. We couldn't have been more different, but, as it turned out, he and I shared something very striking in common.

It began, like the rest, with a message on my computer screen:

Hey Oscar. I hope you don't mind the add.

Unlike the rest, however, Adam took time to crack. The others would get to the point almost instantly. They'd get caught up in the excitement and then beg or threaten me to stay quiet. But tempers and fears were easily subdued with logic:

If I talk, we stop fooling around, and neither of us want that, right?

Boys like logic.

I guessed Adam had more to lose. Social status means a great deal, especially at eighteen. He talked to me for hours on end, almost every night, but he never gave anything away. Not even a hint.

He talked about sports and school and which girls he fancied. Others would do that too, but they'd usually end with something like "but she's so frigid" or "I heard she gives shit head". Something for me to latch onto.

But not Adam. Adam was a real gentleman.

I replied to everything, pretending to care, waiting and waiting for my chance. I asked about his home and his

9

family, about what he wanted to do with his life and where he wanted to go. But it was always just chat.

No leads. Nothing.

Until one Friday. One Friday when I was close to giving up, I learned his parents would be away and he had the place to himself for the weekend. When I asked when his inevitable party would be starting his answer was surprising.

No party.

Why not?

Can't be bothered.

Fair enough. What you gonna do then?

Watch movies. Chill.

Then the little on-screen pen started moving. There was more.

Wanna join?

My heart missed a beat. My cock twitched. Bingo.

Sure. What time?

7?

Sweet.

And it was. Sweeter than sugar. Sweeter than manna from heaven.

Not that I let myself believe it off the bat. I was cautious. Wary. I'd heard horror stories, about guys getting tricked or lured to places. Had my own. So, when I turned up the next night, I watched his house. To make sure he really was alone.

He was. Knock, knock.

I can remember what he was wearing like it was yesterday. Immaculate white sport socks covered his feet, size thirteen at least, heading up and underneath grey tracksuit trousers. The ones that cling in all the right places. To his thick calves and his bulging thighs.

His crotch.

Around his torso was a tight, white t-shirt that fit over his wide pecs like an extra layer of skin. His biceps bulged out either side, supporting two powerful arms, and his shoulders rose like a flawless peak beside his strong neck.

His jaw, square, was smiling, and his blue eyes twinkled under the hallway light. Beautiful blue eyes below a full head of thick, dark brown hair.

'Hey,' he said.

His voice. I'd heard it hundreds of times before. In class, on the field, but never at me. Deep and commanding it reverberated through my body, sending chills down my spine.

I don't remember what I said back, but it must have been funny. He laughed, showing off a full set of gleaming white teeth. Then I remember following him down a narrow hallway, past a small living room and into a kitchen. He got a couple of beers out of a fridge.

I remember watching the vein on his right arm, and his triceps and deltoids tense as he pulled the shiny metal door open. We drank on aluminium stools around a kitchen island, facing each other. Our knees centimetres apart.

I remember the clink of glass as we toasted the weekend. I remember the tour he gave of his house. The sound of the stairs creaking beneath us, the click of a doorknob as he showed me into a bedroom. His bedroom. I remember the double bed, unmade, with a plastic Tupperware box sitting on top.

He asked me if I smoked pot.

'Fuck yeah,' I said.

Picking up and opening the box he sat on the right side of the bed and patted the space next to him. His mattress was firm, not hard, and I could feel the heat of his body down my side.

He smelt good. Too good. I had to fight every urge to touch him. Taste him. I watched his hands instead.

They selected two short rolling papers and turned them so the strips of shiny glue gleamed towards us. Then he lifted them to his mouth. Stuck them together after a single stroke of his tongue. He smiled: I was staring.

Saying nothing he continued, placing the L-shape down and grinding the pungent green before mixing it with tobacco. He rolled it together quickly.

It was textbook. *Expert hands.*

'Here. After you,' he said.

'Piss off,' I said. 'Roller's rights.'

He chuckled, placing the small white spear between his thick lips, and lit it. Breathing in deep he closed his eyes and exhaled, billowing white into the air around us.

He looked like a model as his hand brushed against mine, passing me the smoking stick.

12

'That's what I like about you,' he said.

'You what?' I said after blowing out my own cloud; a gorgeous sticky, gloop beginning to drip through my head already.

'You don't take any shit.'

It was my turn to chuckle. *He came to that conclusion after I smoked second?*

'What's funny?' he said.

'Nothing.'

'Bullshit.'

'Honestly, it's nothing.'

But I couldn't stop: the giggles had got me already. Way quicker than usual. I couldn't believe I was sat next to Adam Stanmore, captain of the rugby team. Smoking his weed. Drinking his beer. In his house. On his bed. And like all laugher, it was contagious.

The rest I'll never forget.

The joking and sniggering as we finished the joint. The play fighting and shoving. The give of his mattress as he pushed me onto it. The smell of his deodorant as he pinned my arms above my head. The weight of his body on mine; him six-foot-six, me six inches shorter.

His pleading stare.

I took my chance. He didn't pull back. Didn't stop me.

Lying between my legs, our cocks hard as stone and grinding against each other under layers of fabric, we kissed.

He was a phenomenal kisser. No wonder all the girls wanted him.

One hand supporting my neck, his thumb caressed my cheek, and the other ran down my chest, my stomach,

13

under my t-shirt and behind onto my back. All the while his tongue glided over mine and explored my mouth.

He tasted like victory.

Releasing his hold his hand joined his other. Gravity pushed him down onto me harder and I threw my arms around his neck. His back tensed as he lifted us away from the mattress with his core and his fingers grabbed my t-shirt. Then, whipping it over my head and breaking my link, we were horizontal again. And I was shirtless.

Expert hands indeed.

Enormous and dominating he knelt over me as the cool air of the room tickled my naked skin. Grinning he pulled up his own shirt. Slowly. Two, four, six-pack. His pecs, hairless and smooth, gleamed like golden silk in the dim lamp light. Throwing the crumpled material to the floor, he remained kneeling.

Licking my lips, I took in every inch of his perfect body through my wide, blue eyes. I followed his V-lines down and under his waistband to his bulge almost ripping open the thin grey cotton. I opened my mouth a fraction.

He got the hint.

Shuffling up towards my face, knee-step by knee-step, his towering figure grew. Bigger and taller until I could smell him: a faint trace of washing detergent mixed with the cum-infused sweat of his crotch.

'You want me to fuck your mouth?' he said.

'Yes.'

A huge hand struck my face. Hard, but not painful. A heat prickled over my cheek. Pre-cum beaded onto my leg.

'Yes, what?' he said.

'Yes, please.'

'Good. Take them down.'

Taking hold of his waistband either side of his thick quads, I peeled downwards. He wasn't wearing any underwear.

Thick, long and straight his cock swung free and landed on my face with a thud. I kept pulling. His balls, big and full swung against my chin.

Without hesitating I licked them into my mouth and rolled them over my tongue. Gently and carefully I gave them the occasional tug, sucking a little harder and revelling in the way his body shuddered.

Thud-thud went his cock as he smacked himself against my cheek.

Opening my mouth, I shifted direction, letting his balls hang against my chin, wet and sticky. I licked him from base to tip. Six inches, seven inches, eight inches, nine, until I felt the satin softness of his head and tasted the saltiness of his pre-cum.

I can't wait any longer.

Grabbing hold I opened my jaw as far as it could go and wrapped my lips around him. He was big. The biggest I'd ever had.

I sucked and sucked, running my hand up and down his shaft as more and more of his pre-cum mixed with my saliva and snaked down my throat. Every taste bud savouring every molecule.

Then, seizing my wrist, he threw my hand away from him and grabbed a tuft of my hair. Pulling me in he drove himself in deeper until his pubes prickled my nostrils. My gag reflex tried to kick in but I didn't let it.

Not with him.

I put my hands on his legs, to steady myself, but he let go of my hair and a vice-like grip tightened around my wrists. My shoulders strained as he lifted my arms above my head, shackled together by one of his hands.

I didn't resist. I didn't want to.

Looking up I watched. Watched him pump in and out of my mouth. In and out. Over and over. His eyes locked on me. You are mine, they said. And I was. I would have let him do anything to me.

He could tell.

Letting go of my wrists he grabbed the back of my head and pushed in the final inch-and-a-half. My throat stretched and my eyes watered as he choked me from the inside, groaning deep and guttural and grinding into my face.

Still holding my breath, I pushed my jeans down and took out my cock. He pulled out, letting me grab a quick gulp of air, but quick it was. He thrusted back in. Built his speed: faster and faster to match the rhythm of my beating hand.

Back and forth, back and forth, I took it like a pro. My lips kissed the base of his stomach each time he smashed against the back of my throat. His balls slapping against my chin. My mouth gurgling and gulping: full.

'Wow,' he said, sliding down so far he pushed tears from my eyes.

Digging my fingers into his arse cheeks he let go of my head. Arching my neck, I took a long, full breath.

For a few seconds he watched me, lying on his bed. Panting. My body shaking and my own muscles tensing as my hand continued to jerk.

A strand of saliva dripped off him and into my open mouth.

'You want my load?' he said.

'Yes please.'

'You gonna blow too?'

'Yes, sir.'

This time he put both hands around my head, lifted me up and let rip. No mercy.

As my tonsils squeezed around him, his breath grew heavier by the second. I felt the blood rush to his cock from inside my mouth. The surge of my own climax began to crescendo. My cock tightened. My hole clenched. My fist pumped as fast as it could.

He pulled back, just in time, and, no hands, blew as my own load hit my abs and poured off in ten different directions. Hot and salty his filled my mouth. It cascaded over my tongue and down towards my stomach. But I closed my throat and let it pool.

Not yet.

Black spots speckled my vision. Blood whirred through my head. My synapses flared into overdrive, flooding my body with pleasure. I closed my lips around him and sucked out every drop.

For what seemed like minutes I unhurriedly licked him clean. His body jolting each time my tongue swept over his tip. Until he could bear the sensitivity no longer.

Pulling out he bent over me and, with two thick fingers, wiped back in a gooey line that had spilled over my cheek. I opened wide and let him play with my mouth. Let him push himself and his load down until his knuckles knocked against my front teeth.

Then, his fingers still inside of me, I swallowed.

Two

Lying on Adam's bed, his gloopy, salty fingers sliding out of my mouth as hundreds of millions of his finest swimmers plummeted to the depths of my stomach, wasn't the last time I'd feel the sharp prickle of fear over my body after taking a load.

But, it's up there with the scariest.

Straightening himself upright his face became partially hidden in darkness. His body tensed. The room went silent. Something primal inside of me jolted awake.

Uh oh.

'What the fuck are you doing, you filthy faggot?' he said.

Now don't get me wrong, I'd heard those words before. Especially the last one.

Those delightful six letters had always managed to find their way to my ears at break or lunch, or from cars of lads to and from school.

And online.

I'd quickly learned that the chat windows were also a place for boys to hang their dirty laundry. Stop the stains of insecurity from stinking out their minds by directing their fear and anger at me.

Especially after they'd had their fun. When reality would come crashing back and their sordid fantasies were inescapable black facts on white screens.

As I've said before, logic's your friend in these situations, gift-wrapped in straight boy slang and guarantees. But without the QWERTY line of defence it was infinitely more confronting. Particularly when the guy in question was my size and a half, height and width, with fists like bricks and pinning me down with his entire body.

Think. Carefully.

And what's that they say about fight and flight? When you can't do one you do the other, right?

In an instant, my upper lip raised in a snarl. Adrenaline pumped through my veins and my fists clenched. My eyes darted to his flesh. He was close enough that I could sink my teeth into somewhere very sensitive and very delicate and he would not want to clamp my jaw any tighter.

But a lot can happen in half a second of reaction time. He could move. He could punch me before I even tried.

If I can do maximum damage before the carnage to my face begins, I'll wake happy. If I wake.

To my relief it was all for nothing. Adam, it seemed, liked to play games. And I should have seen it coming really. He was the captain of the rugby team.

'Get the fuck off me,' I said.

'Whoa, Oscar, buddy, I'm kidding.'

'Don't call me buddy.'

'Look, honestly, I'm joking.'

And he was. Or at least, when he gently pushed me back onto the mattress, shuffled towards my feet, put two hands either side of my waist and licked every one of my load-coated abs clean with his wide, flat tongue, it was a pretty convincing performance.

'Trust me now?' he said looking up with a glazed grin before wiping his mouth with the back of his hand.

In the panic, I'd momentarily forgotten where and who I was with. But from that angle, in the lamplight, past my chest rising and falling slower and slower as my heart calmed and my extra testosterone fizzled into embarrassment, I remembered.

Adam was very handsome. His eyes were stunning. They really had been twinkling under the light in his hallway. And while in the gentle glow of his bedroom the blue was almost gone, the gleam was not.

I can't stay angry at that face, no matter how stupid it is.

And he'd missed a spot.

'You've still got some on you,' I said, sitting up, leaning in, putting a hand around his neck and pulling him down so I could kiss his lower lip clean.

Then I punched him in the stomach.

Tensing his powerful abs, he effortlessly stopped my fist in its tracks. Grinned.

'I deserved that,' he said.

Pushing me back down and himself backwards to standing he pulled his tracksuit trousers back up, whipping the waistband against himself. His deflating cock still making an impressive mound.

For a minute, we said nothing. Him standing. Me sitting. Him still grinning like an idiot. Me savouring his flavour all through my mouth; on my tongue, between my teeth, around my gums. Both shirtless. Both pleased with ourselves.

I broke the silence by picking up his box of goodies.

Click-click went the plastic blue fasteners on each side of the lid. From the smell, I could tell it was good

20

weed. Sickly sweet it crumbled nicely between my fingers. I rolled a joint, sat up against his headboard and lit it.

'Almost as good as mine,' he said, sliding in next to me through the fresh haze.

Our bare shoulders and feet touched. Our faces forward, staring at the black screen of a TV on top of a clothes chest. Various items strewn sloppily over open drawers.

'In your wet dreams,' I said, passing the joint before draining the dregs of my beer I'd put on the bedside table.

It was warm but still tasty. Everything at Adam's was.

'For a moment, I thought you were going to beat the shit out of me,' I said.

'Yeah, I'm sorry. It was stupid.'

'It's alright. It was kind of funny.'

'Yeah?'

'Kind of. In hindsight.'

'Yeah, sorry again.'

'All good, man.'

He passed the joint back and I took two full drags. We kept eye contact the whole time.

'I wasn't expecting that,' I said.

'What? You and me?'

'No. I knew that would happen.'

'Fuck off.'

'Come on, of course I did.'

'How?'

'It's not like I predicted the exact outcome, but do you really think you're the only guy to add me on MSN since everyone found out–'

'You suck dick in bowling alley toilets?'

Taking a long drag, I held it in for three counts and blew, slowly, in his face. He didn't move. Didn't flinch. Just stared, smirking through the sticky fog a foot from my lips, until I passed him the joint again.

'He sucked my dick, alright?' I said. 'But yeah, since everyone found out. I didn't expect you to be so cool with it.'

'Cool with what?'

'Being like me.'

'Like you?'

'Being a filthy faggot.'

'Oh. Right.'

'Yeah. Most guys aren't as ok with it. They're nervous. It's hot. Sometimes.'

I laughed and turned, but he wasn't smiling. He looked sad. Taking two more drags, he dropped the joint in his finished bottle of beer. The sizzle of the extinguishing cherry in the remaining dregs echoed up the neck and lingered in the air alongside its final wisps of heavy grey.

'I'm not gay,' he said.

'Sure you're not,' I said gesturing to my stomach, crusting slightly under an invisible layer of dried saliva and cum.

'I'm not,' he said turning to face me.

He rested his head in his hand, propped up by his elbow. His bicep like a boulder of muscle.

'I'm bi,' he said.

'Really?'

'What's that supposed to mean?'

'You're not the first guy to tell me *that* either.'

Although, in his defence, he was the first I believed.

I'm not entirely sure why. Call it intuition, or a gut reaction. Pun intended. Or maybe it was just the look in his eyes. Lost. Unsure.

A minority in a minority.

Shifting my position, I matched his. On my side, facing him. Our noses almost touching. He said nothing.

'You alright?' I said.

'No one's ever going to believe me.'

'I believe you.'

'No you don't.'

'Adam, mate, I do. I'm sorry I didn't take you seriously but come on, can you blame me?'

'I suppose not.'

'Why so sad?'

'I'm not sad. It's just fucked up. If two girls get it on they're not automatically branded dykes for the rest of their lives. But if a guy so much as touches another lad then he's just gay. That's it. Nothing else.'

'It's not so bad, you know? Who the fuck wants to be a sheep anyway?'

'You wouldn't understand.'

Get a grip you fucking pussy, is what I'd wanted to say. Even though I didn't blame any of them for staying in the closet, it didn't mean I had any patience when they came bitching about their lives to me.

I didn't get the luxury of coming out. It was forced on me.

Instead I said, 'Society's fucked up, man.'

'True.'

'So when did you know?'

'That I liked guys too?'

'Yeah.'

'Remember Mr. Price?' he said.

Time suddenly stood still. For the briefest fraction of a moment but I felt it through my whole body.

Mr. Price?

'How could I forget?' I said.

How could anyone forget Mr. Price is Right? Hands down the sexiest sports teacher our school had ever had. Potentially the most handsome man I'd ever seen.

Six-foot-three, early thirties, hairy legs always, always on show under tiny rugby shorts come rain, hail, snow or shine. Shaved head, brown eyes, strong jaw, big arms.

Perfection.

Then one day, he'd gone crazy. Literally started screaming at a year seven boy in front of the whole school for next to no reason. No one had known why or what had made him snap so suddenly.

Or so I'd thought.

'Right?' he said.

'No!'

He nodded, sucking in air between his teeth. Envy punching me in the stomach. Hard.

'You lucky fucker. When?' I said.

'Year eleven.'

'What, you were fifteen?'

'Sixteen.'

'You looked about twenty-one,' I said. 'Still do.'

He winked. Nudged me with his shoulder.

'At first he was just a good teacher. I was already his height and still growing so he must have known I was a natural for the game. He'd give me extra pointers after school and drive me home. To be honest I thought he fancied my mum.'

But?

'But then one afternoon after practice, I got a phone call. My grandad had tripped and was in hospital. He was fine, just a few scratches and bruises, but when I got back to the changing rooms there was no one there except him.'

I pictured it. Row after row of metal benches in a misty, muddy room. White tiled walls glistening with condensation from the showers. Mr Price's office in the far-right corner.

I'd played rugby before, back when sport had been a compulsory subject. I knew how the room would have looked. How it would have smelt. How it would have felt: the heat from twenty or so sweaty boys still radiating like fog.

'He was at his computer with his back to me. He didn't hear me come in so I started to get undressed. Then I heard a woman moaning.'

'Porn.'

'Got it in one. He was jerking off.'

'What I would give,' I said, meaning every, single, word.

'Mate, it gets better.'

'I'm all ears.'

His eyes lit up. He probably hadn't told this story to anyone before and he was loving it. And so was I. With empty balls, my cock still twitched eagerly under my Calvin Kleins.

'Back then I already knew there was something different about me. I was into girls, but sometimes in the showers I'd see one or two of the lads and I'd start getting. You know.'

'Yeah. I do.'

'So, I crept forward like a ninja. I only had shorts on, so it was easy. I got to the door frame and watched. I could see it all. The bird on the screen getting fucked from behind. Mr. Price with his rugby shorts by his ankles, his t-shirt to his nipples, his cock in his hand. It was beautiful.'

'How big was he?'

'I don't know in inches but he was big. Bigger than me and mine was almost full size back then I assure you.'

'I wouldn't doubt it in a million years.'

Adam smiled and winked.

'You like this story?' he said.

I did. *Big time*.

'It's alright,' I said.

'There's more.'

'I won't stop you.'

'I watched. For ages. It probably wasn't even a minute but it felt like hours. I was transfixed. I'd never dared to even look at gay porn and there I was, metres away from Mr. fucking Price about to blow a nut all over himself. And then, just when I thought he was about to shoot, he stopped, paused the video and, without turning, said, "I know you're there".'

'No fucking way.'

'Yes fucking way.'

'What did you do?'

'I froze, like a statue. I considered grabbing my stuff and running, but I couldn't move. Thank fuck I didn't because by the time my feet started working he reached over to the spare chair with his free hand and pulled it next to him.'

I knew exactly which chair Adam was talking about. I'd sat on it.

I'd only been inside his office once: he'd caught me ditching PE. I did it all the time, but I'd been lazy. Or maybe I'd let him see me. Maybe I'd wanted his gaze to fall on me for once.

He'd been sat in this expensive, black orthopaedic chair and I remember sitting less than half a metre from him. Opposite his phenomenal body in his futuristic thrown. His cool and calm demeanour. Collected. In charge.

I'd been inches from him and mesmerised. Sat in awe on the uncomfortable, green fabric, rickety spare and wishing and yearning I was on his.

On him.

'He wanted you to join,' I said.

'Yup. He pulled it over and patted the top. Didn't say a word.'

'Tell me you joined him.'

'Without a doubt! I didn't hesitate. I walked over and sat down. He didn't even look at me, he just pressed play.'

'Fuck.'

'Yeah it was hot. So hot. I kept looking at him from the corner of my eyes, but he never took his off the screen. He just pumped and pumped as this chick with giant tits got smashed by some guy with tatts.'

'Shame.'

'That's what I thought. Until he was about to blow.'

'What happened?'

'His breath started getting heavier and his legs started tensing. At this point it could have been EastEnders on the screen, I wasn't watching. I was watching him. Watching his muscles flex and his arm work like a piston.'

'Fuck.'

'Then he started making these deep, throaty grunts and I knew what was coming.'

I closed my eyes and I could see him. Hear him. His shaved head rolling back on his huge shoulders. His chest filling with air. Every muscle in his legs and arms swelling.

'Before he blew, he reached across with his free hand and clamped it on my leg. Then he turned, stared straight into my eyes, dug his fingers and thumb into my quad as hard as he could and unloaded himself all over his stomach.'

My cock ached to be free. Free from my jeans and in my hand. Pre-cum soaking through my underwear to my leg.

'How big was his load?' I said.

'Huge. It shot out of him and kept on pouring. It went all the way up to his stomach and on his shirt but he didn't care. He just squeezed my leg harder and harder, staring at me.'

For a minute neither of us said anything. We were lost in images.

I was savouring every second of his story. Knowing exactly how it would have played out. Adam no doubt relishing a memory relived. A secret shared from a past still hidden.

It was his turn to break the silence.

'Oscar, I'm hard as a rock.'

'Me too.'

'What shall we do?'

'I have a few ideas,' I said.

Three

Boys who like boys like boys who like boys.

Sounds simple, right?

Think about them for a moment. Eighteen-year-old lads like Adam and myself. Full of energy. Ever-growing creatures of mystery, muscle and testosterone. Going through changes, both mental and physical. Emerging into manhood is normal. It's natural.

Like they've done since childhood they'll question it. What, why, how do we understand these changes in our hair-sprouting, sweaty bodies?

We do what everyone must do to learn. We experiment. We experience.

You'd think, then, with hormones flying and adolescent heights to scale, when two boys who like boys are in bed together, engines fired and imaginations infinite, they'd soar as high and as hot as they can.

Think again.

Life isn't like the movies. And it certainly isn't like porn. Yes, it wasn't difficult to get my co-pilot, Adam, to feed me an inflight appetiser and spin me some dinner entertainment, but, the main course was still a blip on the horizon.

The problem was, most boys who like boys at that age, that electrifying and terrifying age of adulthood, don't know how to fire the engines and fly. And, while most of them have seen many an on-screen demonstration, novices often get apprehensive around the knobs and buttons.

I could tell by the fear in his eyes and the trepidation in his voice, Adam was going to be no different. Fortunately, I wasn't like most boys. I'd had a lot of practice in the cockpit.

'Well?' he said.

His eyes were still wide with anticipation. His cock really was as hard as a rock under the thin, grey fabric of his tracksuit trousers, stretching across his entire leg. But so was mine, aching to be free of my denim.

Time to prepare for take-off.

Sitting up against the headboard, I narrowed my eyes and fixed my gaze. Only his moved. They followed me. His chiselled face, illuminated by the bedside lamp, remained still. Propped up in his strong hand at the end of his sculpted forearm.

'Did Mr. Price ever do what I just did?' I said.

Above a mischievous grin, his stare, animated and excited, lingered for a second more. From my angle, the colour was back with a vengeance. His eyes sparkled again. Then they flicked down to his crotch.

'Many times,' he said, running his palm from the tip of his cock, wrapped in cotton, down to the base.

Closing his hand around himself he squeezed. His whole body tensed. A long, thick vein bulged along his bicep.

'Good memories?' I said.

He looked back up. His eyes searing blue in the light.

'Some of the best.'

'Who was better?'

'You.'

I grinned. *Good answer.*

Although, from the way Adam had worked my throat, I hadn't needed to ask my first question. It was superfluous. I could tell mine wasn't the only mouth he'd fucked that didn't usually have lipstick around it. Unless teenage girls were suddenly into rough deepthroat.

Unlikely.

But, the next question. That mattered.

'Did you suck his?' I said.

Letting a dude suck you off is one thing. Sucking one off is another. Some of the so-called straights had gotten quite uptight when it came to choking down a few inches. And in my case, more than a few.

'Yes,' Adam said.

'Did you like it?'

He looked down again. At me.

'I fucking loved it.'

An even better answer. Clearly Mr. Price had taught Adam more than how to ruck and scrum.

'Good,' I said.

Unfastening my belt, I pulled the two ends apart. The buckle slumped onto my leg with a clink and I undid the top button of my jeans.

'Help a brother out?' I said.

'You want me to suck your cock?'

'Be a good boy.'

Recollection flickered in his eyes like I'd hoped it would. He'd heard those words before.

Shifting his weight, he rolled onto his front, over one of my legs, so his torso rested between them. Running his hands up the outside of my thighs to the top of my arse, he supported himself by his elbows.

His mouth was only inches from my crotch. His feet, over the end of the bed, lifted toward me until his soles pointed to the ceiling. His bare back looked phenomenal, tensed in all the right places, down to two hidden but almost spherical arse cheeks.

Licking his lips, he pinched the tiny gold rectangle at the end of my zip and pulled. Tooth by tooth the metal unclasped until two flaps of denim splayed open, revealing a layer of thin white cotton stretched over my hard cock.

He took a deep breath, no doubt savouring the sight and smells in front of him. Looking up he watched me intently. He was waiting.

He is a good boy.

'Now pull down my jeans. Slowly.'

Without a word, he grasped my waistband with both hands and peeled my jeans down. The bunching material forced my legs closer together. Sliding my feet up the bed, I lifted my knees up and to the side, away from his head. With one last pull, denim, metal and leather hit the floor.

Opening my legs, I lowered them to their previous positions either side of him. The room was warm, but the air tickled my freshly naked skin. Clenching, I raised my cock beneath its tight restraints.

'He wants to be free,' he said.

'He does,' I said. 'Pass the weed.'

'How will I smoke?' he said, handing me the box.

He looked cute when he was confused.

'I'm going to smoke. You're going to suck.'

He smiled, raised his eyebrows and said, 'Ok.'

He was enjoying our little role reversal.

'I'm going to ask you some questions,' I said.

'What about?'

32

Pulling down the band of my undies with one hand I pulled out my cock with the other. For a second he went cross-eyed: his vision refocusing on something big and new and close. His mouth hung open.

'I'm asking the questions,' I said, releasing my underwear and putting my now free hand on the back of his head.

I pulled him towards me. He didn't resist. My cock pulsed with imminent anticipation in my other hand.

His hair tickling my fingers, I felt the wet heat of his mouth wrap around me. My arse tensed, my hole clenched, my body shuddered and a short breathy gasp forced its way out of my mouth.

His tongue, smooth and slippery, glided across the underside of my shaft, up and around my head. I let go, of him and myself, and leaned into the pillows bundled against the headboard behind me.

For five long minutes, I left him to enjoy himself as I rolled a joint. At first, he was careful and considerate, which I appreciated. The last thing you want is a toothy amateur going gun's blazing.

He made sure his lip covered his top front teeth and his tongue covered the sharp canines below. He opened his jaw wide enough to fit me in but didn't lose suction. I was impressed. He was a total gentleman.

Until he found his rhythm and his eyes rolled to the back of his head. Until his inner cocksucker came out. Then, jerking, licking, savouring and kissing, he was in heaven.

And so was I. On a scale of one to ten, one being your dick comes out bleeding and ten being you blow so hard you cum out his nose, Adam was a solid eight. Truth be told, there were occasions when I had to stop rolling and surrender to the waves of pleasure lapping at my balls.

He's definitely done this before.

Finished rolling, I lit the joint and inhaled deeply. He slowed down and watched me. Watched me hold the heavy, blissful drag as I stared back into his eyes. My head swimming with a growing layer of fresh THC. My body tingling thanks to his thick, eager lips attached to his hungry, eager mouth.

I exhaled into the air and counted to ten in my head, his tongue dancing around the head of my cock. Then I spoke.

'So,' I said.

He stopped sucking and looked up: his cheek pushed out from the inside. It was a good look on him. Lifting his head, he released me from his mouth with a slurp. My cock catapulted backwards and slapped against the base of my abs.

'So?' he mimicked.

'So tell me. What else do you fucking love to do?'

'I dunno. What do you like to do?'

Breathing out a cloud of smoke in his face, I grabbed my cock in my free hand and slapped it against his cheek.

'What did I say about asking questions?'

He smiled.

'I fucking love to fuck,' he said.

'Who doesn't?'

He said nothing. He was learning.

'But we've got all night,' I continued. 'Surely there's something else you'd like to do?'

He looked down and to the side. His fingers absentmindedly playing with the bedsheet.

34

I couldn't believe it, Adam Stanmore, captain of the rugby team and King of School, had gone all shy.

'It's ok. You can tell me,' I said.

'There's one thing I've never done,' he said. 'Mr. Price wanted me to do it to him, once, but I didn't want to.'

'Why not?'

'I don't know. I don't think I was ready.'

'Are you ready now?'

'I think so. With you.'

'Lucky me.'

'I've thought about doing it ever since you gave your presentation in English. I just wanted to bend you over Miss Stephenson's desk.'

Taking a final drag of the joint, I dropped it into our beer bottle ashtray. It sizzled to an end next to the others. My cock, hard and gooey, bounced on my stomach.

I knew exactly what he was about to say.

'Mate. You can definitely do that to me,' I said.

'You don't even know what I want.'

'Ask me then.'

He eyed my cock.

'Don't worry. You're safe,' I said with a wink.

'Can I rim you?'

Got it in one.

No wonder he hadn't wanted to stick his tongue up Mr. Price's hole. Don't get me wrong, I would have happily buried my face deep between those glorious peaks, but when you're young and confused and used to hairless pussies in your face, it's not exactly the first thing you'd go for.

'Fuck yes,' I said.

'It's all … ok down there?'

Remember what I said about them being apprehensive around the equipment? Case in point.

'You mean will you get shit in your mouth?' I said.

He laughed. Nervously. Said, 'You really don't mess around do you?'

'No. And no, you won't. I'm clean as a whistle.'

'How do you know?'

I smiled. *Poor innocent, uninitiated boy.* As if I hadn't come prepared.

Not that I blamed him. I'd felt the same way when I'd been less experienced. Until I'd met a silver fox in my early days of Gaydar.

He used to pick me up in his Mercedes and drive me to a penthouse room at the Hilton in the city. He'd let me use the big bath for as long as I wanted and order champagne and strawberries to the room. Then, spotless, I would lie on my stomach on the king-size bed with my face in plush hotel pillows and he'd eat me out for hours.

That guy had taught me a few lessons about sexual upkeep. After the first time I'd douched, I couldn't believe how good I'd tasted on his lips.

I smacked Adam in the face with my cock again. His saliva had congealed and it struck his cheek with a slap.

'Trust me,' I said.

Glaring at me, he wiped away the gunk with the back of his hand. Neither of us said anything. I could almost hear the cogs in his head turning.

Then they stopped.

Pulling my briefs down and off in the same motion he threw them across the room. Then, putting my feet soles-down on the bed, I sat myself up. My cock flopped on to the duvet and my balls hung below. The V of my naked legs ran either side of his head.

Lifting himself up, he kneeled in front of me and wrapped his hands around each of my shins; his fingertips digging into my calves. Pushing me back until my shoulders rocked against the headboard, he lifted my arse. My cheeks spread.

He looked at my hole. I couldn't see but I knew I was hairless. I'd been looking forward to Adam's house all day and I'd come prepared.

'Ok,' he said. 'I trust you.'

'Then let rip.'

Four

We all have those moments. Moments we wish lasted longer.

What happened next, on Adam's bed is one of them: the split-second moment before his hot tongue sent ripples of ecstasy through my body.

It was the look in his eyes. The soft curve of his smile. The gentle dip in room volume as he took a breath and held it.

He was no longer just one half of a horny duo. He was that, certainly, but he was more. He was a social anomaly too. Accepted without judgement. He wasn't just Adam, rugby captain and King of School. He was Adam, cock-sucker-soon-to-be-arse-rimmer.

And proud.

In a thump of a heartbeat, he was finally being himself and doing what he'd dreamt of. And I know now I was lucky to be a part of it.

But not at the time. I was oblivious to any deeper meaning. Both of us were: neither of us recognised any significance. We were kids. And, like I said, it wasn't love between us.

It was freedom, and at that age, it's too easy to take freedom for granted.

Ironic, seeing as, stuck in a town in the middle of an overcrowded island, with my hole winking up at a sexually frustrated, testosterone-fuelled rugby player, I was physically and psychologically far from free.

I was utterly dominated and I loved it.

Yanking my legs toward him he effortlessly pulled me down the bed, away from the headboard. The cotton of the sheets whispered as my back swept over it. He could have thrown me around like a leaf if he'd wanted to.

Even if I resist he can.

Instead he wedged his hands under my knees and pushed my legs until the fronts of my thighs touched the bed alongside my torso. My calves folded towards him and locked his grips in place. He smiled and raised his eyebrows.

Impressed.

'Is that all you've got?' I said.

A devilish grin crept up into face and seeped into his eyes. I recognised it. He'd worn it pumping his cock down my throat.

His hold tightened. The veins on his arms swelled. He had more.

Relaxing my lower body, I let him compress me until my arse pointed to the ceiling. I clenched my hole as tight as I could. Even though I could scratch my head with my knees, I still needed to be as tight as possible.

The more you clench, the better it feels when his tongue pushes you open. And there's aesthetics to think about.

'Wow,' he said.

In all fairness, I'd checked before leaving the house. One of the many advantages of having a mirror facing your bed is bending yourself over and pulling your cheeks apart to ensure you're looking your best.

It's a pity there isn't one in here.

Straightening his legs out behind him, he lowered himself down in a push-up motion. His body weight shifted through me, straining the springs below us.

Lying flat on his stomach he held my legs in position. It was nothing for his humongous arms.

He lowered his head, showing off his thick, chestnut brown crown. My hole rose to meet him and his breath was warm against me. Chills shot over my skin.

He froze and looked up. His blue eyes piercing into mine. His lips quivering inches from my hole, served on a platter in front of him.

What now?

'I've never done this before,' he said.

I know.

'It's ok,' I said gently. 'Take your time. Enjoy yourself.'

Three seconds passed.

Patience, Oscar.

'What does it taste like?' he said.

If I didn't know rolling my eyes would kill the mood they would have rolled out my head and onto the floor. *Now's not the time for a fucking Q&A.* I was happy to keep this position for as long as necessary but it wasn't for a heart to heart.

'Like skin,' I said.

'Really?'

'Sweaty skin. With a hint of metal,' I said with a wink.

'Metal?'

'From all the blood vessels.'

'Oh.'

I could tell he still didn't understand: biology probably not his strongest subject at school. But I'd already

40

lost patience. Instead, reaching up between my legs, I ran my fingers through his hair. Curled a few strands in my fingers and let them go. Then I ran the backs of my fingers down his smooth cheek.

'Besides,' I said, pinching his chin between my thumb and index finger. 'It's not just the taste, it's the texture. It's like eating pussy. But better.'

He nodded and his stare relaxed. He looked down again and I followed his eyes. They were taking me in. My hairless pecs. My fat-less folded abdomen. My hard cock almost poking me in the nipple. My balls hanging backwards. My legs spread. My hole.

Clunk-clunk went his head cogs. Decision made.

And what a decision. Considering the false start, I assumed he would be like most rimming virgins. Slow and careful; kissing and licking the peripheral; slyly breathing as much scent and tasting as much flavour as possible to discern the terrifying, new territory. But not Adam

Finally convinced, he lived up to his moniker of king and went for glory.

His large, flat tongue squashed strong against me and ran from the tip of my tail bone up, over my hole, to the bottom of my rigid cock. My body, pinned firmly down, still managed to roll as a wave of ecstasy undulated towards my head, cracking vertebrae on the way.

My head thumped into the doughy white of his pillow. Blood rushed to my hole and my cock. The room, hazy and grey from our smoke, span a full three-sixty as my crack tingled hot to suddenly cold. He'd pulled back: millions of his saliva molecules evaporating away my body heat into the air.

I watched him, down, past my contorted body. He was looking at me. Now his eyes flickered with excitement, and behind closed lips, his tongue moved through his mouth.

He was tasting me. Like wine. He swallowed.

'Well?' I said.

'Well what?' he said still smirking.

I said nothing. I had no point to prove.

I always taste good.

Arching my neck, I put my hands behind my head. He matched my speed. As the backs of my hands met his pillow, his tongue met the constricted walls of my hole.

Like bare wires touching, each tightly packed bundle of nerve fibres jolted into action, firing a loud moan into my stomach, through my lungs and into the room.

Finally able to unclench, I fully surrendered. One-hundred percent malleable my knees pushed a final inch into the bed and his tongue drove inside of me.

Every hair on my arms and legs stood on end. His hands clasped tighter above, or from that angle, below my knees. He moaned into me and my cock shuddered. Pre-cum dribbled onto myself, squeezed out by his vibrations.

I closed my eyes as he forced me open again and again. Darkness descended and my other senses took over. My breath grew heavier, taking in the sweet saltiness of our bodies. Visions of him doing everything I could imagine danced through my mind to the rhythm and sounds of his hot, wet muscle.

For how long he spread me open and ate my arse I have no idea. I fell into a sexual blackout. All I know is he took my advice. He took his time and enjoyed himself. Didn't waste a second.

He pressed and prodded and probed, licking and kissing and slurping between my cheeks. Eventually he moved his hands down, sweeping his thumbs over and

42

under so he could hold me open wider. Cool air tickled my insides as my hole gaped open for a second before he plugged me with his tongue again.

'Oh god,' I croaked, unable to stifle praise for the present. 'Oh my fucking god.'

Reaching out in the blackness, I found the back of his head and pulled him into me harder. I opened my eyes. To watch. But the sting of lamplight slammed them shut again. Shielding my vision with my other arm I fixed my aching retinas on him.

He was stunning. It all was. My own biceps and triceps bulging as I held him down. His fingers digging into my thighs either side of my crotch. His nose squashed into the base of my cock. The tops of his wet cheeks glistening.

I couldn't see his lips but I could tell he was smiling. I saw it in his eyes, staring at me over the ridge of my gooch.

Everything is going to plan.

Letting go of his head I put both hands on his shoulders and gave them a deep squeeze. His muscles were knotted and he reacted exactly how I'd expected a sportsman accustom to remedial massage, legitimate or not, would.

He stopped eating, his jaw hung and then a long, deep breath blasted over me as he savoured the release.

'I thought you said don't stop,' he said, speaking into my hole.

'I have an idea.'

He looked up. He liked my ideas.

I tapped his wrist with my knuckle twice. Time to let go. With one last push, he propelled himself backwards and up to kneeling.

Unfolding and straightening my legs I stretched before rolling up to sitting. He watched me, naked, shuffle towards the headboard. I watched him. His wide chest rose and fell. His hairless but powerful abs shimmered slightly with sweat. His cock tented his tracksuit trousers. He wiped his mouth and I laughed.

'What?' he said.

I looked down. At his tent.

'Those are a bit pointless, don't you think?' I said.

'Any excuse to get me naked.'

Leap frogging up he stood his entire six feet six inches. Still watching me he finished undressing. Peeling the stretchy grey fabric down, he released his cock.

Now mouth-level it bounced. Up and down, jutting from a flawlessly defined groin. He rolled off his white sport socks one by one.

Everything about him was proportionate. His body was basically perfect. His cock *was* perfect. Sweet wafts of my dried spit mixed with his load reached my nostrils and my mouth watered. I wanted to wrap my lips around him again. Feel my throat stretch.

But it's my other hole's turn.

'I want you to fuck me,' I said.

His grin reappeared.

'But not here,' I said.

'Why? What's wrong with here?'

Rocking myself forward I sat on the edge of the bed. He didn't move.

'I want to watch.'

He made a confused face.

'What, like, film it?' he said.

I kissed his cock. *So stupid.*

'Not quite,' I said.

44

'Then what?'

I kissed him a second time. *So adorable.*

'How do you think?' I said.

It took two seconds. One: his brow unfurrowed. Two: his eyes brightened.

'Naughty,' he said.

'That's my middle name.'

'There's one in my parents' room.'

'How big?'

'Massive.'

'When do they get back?'

'Tomorrow night.'

I kissed him a third time.

'Excellent,' I said.

'There's one in the living room too.'

'Which is closer?'

'Parents'.'

I looked at his bedside table.

'I'm guessing they don't use condoms?' I said.

'Gross.'

'Sorry, but you're not fucking me raw.'

'Why not?'

'You're just not, alright?'

He opened his mouth to speak but stopped. He knew there was no point in pushing it. Instead he reached down, opened the bedside table and pulled out a strip of blue metallic packets. XXL was printed above the brand in bold, white letters.

'I've got lube too,' he said.

Reaching behind my back I wiped my middle finger between my cheeks and lifted it up to him. Gooey, it glinted in the light.

'I think we're good for lube,' I said.

He smirked, bent over and sucked my finger clean.

'You have an answer for everything, don't you?'

It was my turn to flash an evil grin.

'Not everything,' I said.

'Oh yeah. What don't you know?'

'Plenty.'

'Like what?'

Standing I looked deep into his eyes. Taking one of his hands I placed it on my arse. His fingers slipped between my cheeks and rested against my hole. Standing on tip toes I kissed him.

'I don't know where your parents' room is.'

Five

I got my answer in fifteen seconds.

One: he smiled. Two: he squeezed my arse. Three: he took my hand. Four: I followed.

Five, six, seven: he led me out of his bedroom. Eight, nine, ten: down the hallway. Eleven: he faced me. Twelve: he winked. Thirteen: he reached behind and grabbed the door knob. Fourteen: click.

Fifteen.

'If your parents could see you now,' I said.

'Don't even,' he said, turning the dimmer switch and filling the room with a faint glow.

The room was no larger than his but even through the low light everything was different. The furniture. The temperature. The smell as pristine as its appearance.

The perfect place to get filthy.

Walking us inside he pulled over a framed photograph standing on a chest of drawers with his other hand. Glass rattled inside metal as it clapped against polished wood.

'Mum and Dad?'

'Worse,' he said. 'Grandparents.'

I pulled a sarcastic face. Said, 'They wouldn't approve?'

Sitting down facing me on the immaculately-made queen-size bed, he propped himself up with locked arms.

The mattress gave only slightly under his impressive weight and I smiled to myself.

Firm is always better.

Walking forward I stood between his thick, strong legs. Behind him a floor-to-ceiling mirrored wardrobe reflected us in two wide panels. My torso rose out of his gigantic shoulders and his crew-cut head was in line with my sternum. His back looked fantastic, but his cock, still rock hard, rose upwards, resting against his thigh.

The view directly in front was better though. *For now.*

'I wouldn't know. They died before I was born,' he said.

'Sorry,' I said, backing off half a step. 'Way to kill the mood, hey?'

'It's ok,' he said, reaching out and pulling me back towards him by my waist.

His wide hands were warm against my skin. Thoughts of being thrown onto the bed or floor or up against the wall raced through my head and tugged between my legs.

'I never met them. It's my parents you should worry about,' he said.

'Oh yeah?' I said, turning my body from side to side so my cock knocked against his arms.

I wanted to change the subject. The mood needed lightening. Talking about his family wasn't what I'd had in mind.

Problem was, it wasn't my mind I had to worry about.

'My dad said if he ever caught me with a girl in his bed he would kill me. I'm pretty sure he'd kill us both if he found out.'

48

I laughed. *The old man would have to catch me first.*

'As if you've never fucked anyone in their bed,' I said.

He tightened his grip on my waist and a spasm of ticklishness lurched through me.

'I haven't,' he said.

'Bullshit,' I said, flicking his ear.

'Why's it so hard to believe?'

'I don't get invited to your parties but I've heard about them.'

He smiled, but shrugged it straight off. In all the years of watching him, in the classroom, by the lockers, after school, it wasn't like Adam Stanmore to be modest.

'Half true. But this room's off limits,' he said.

'Lucky me.'

'You think so?'

'I know so.'

Running his hands down to my hips he followed with his eyes. My cock twitched in anticipation but he let go. Something was up.

'Not if they find out,' he said.

'They won't.'

'They might.'

Putting my arms around his neck I sat on his left leg and examined his face. I was right. No smile. No cheeky grin. Only a blank stare.

I shot a look down. His cock was semi-hard. I was losing him.

'So what if they do?' I said gently, lifting his chin with my finger and looking into his eyes; a deeper fear prickling across their surfaces. 'It wouldn't be the end of the world.'

'It's not as simple as that.'

'Nothing ever is. But it's alright,' I said.

'No, it isn't.'

'What makes you say that?'

'I don't know if I can do this.'

My jaw dropped. Only slightly, but I couldn't help it. Blood rushed to my face and anger boiled in my stomach. Disbelief clouding my thoughts.

After all this. After all the hours I've put in reading his bitching and moaning on MSN. After everything we just did he's pussying out now?

Thankfully, I've never been one for giving up without exhausting every avenue. Softening my face, I smiled and counted another four reps in my head.

Slowly, slowly catchy monkey.

'It's ok, mate. Honestly, it's fine,' I said getting off my perch and sitting down on the bed next to him.

'Really?'

'Of course. I'll go.'

'No, please don't. Stay.'

I nodded. Reverse psychology. Like a big-dicked daddy it's an oldie but a goodie.

'If you don't want to do anything else that's cool as well,' I said.

'No I want to. Fuck, Oscar, I really want to bu–'

'Your parents. I know.'

'Fuck them. I couldn't give a toss what they think. They're never around to give a shit about what I do anyway.'

'I know the feeling,' I said.

'You do?'

'Yeah.'

50

Turning his neck, he looked at me and I caught his eyes. Like the confused, bisexual teenager he was, all kinds of emotions whirled in his sapphire spheres. Anger, anxiety, sadness, dread.

But there was excitement too. It flashed across his irises up into his eyebrows, raising them by a fraction of a centimetre.

'Can I tell you something?' he said.

Smiling I held up my hands in a shrug position and looked my own naked body up and down.

'What do you think?' I said.

'Seriously, you can't say a word. He could get into serious trouble.'

'Who?'

'Mr. Price.'

Whether or not Adam noticed my eyes light up is hard to say, but there's no denying they did. We may have reached a temporary road block on our journey, but Mr. Price was a detour I was more than willing to take.

But why bring it up?

'Are you fucking serious? Your parents caught you and *him*?' I said.

'God no,' he said. 'He'd already be in prison. Or dead.'

'Then what?'

'It was his wife. She caught us. In their bed.'

'Oh. Shit.'

'It was awful.'

'What happened?'

He shuffled uncomfortably, and, slowly stroking his own arm, took a deep breath.

'It was a Saturday afternoon, about two months after the changing rooms. We'd been doing stuff ever since. Not fucking or anything. Stuff.'

'Like what?'

'Jerking off. At first. School was too risky so after practice he'd drive us out near the woods before taking me home.'

'Hot.'

He shot me a look. This wasn't that kind of story. To him.

'Sorry,' I said. *Touchy*, I thought. 'How often did you meet?'

'After every practice.'

'Three times a week?'

'Four if you count match days.'

'Wow.'

'It was intense. I couldn't concentrate at school. I stopped caring about rugby. All I wanted was to get in his car.'

'I don't blame you.'

Letting out a single, breathy laugh he nudged me with his shoulder. The corner of his mouth raised in a small smile.

'I was terrified. I loved it, but I had no idea what the hell was going on. We never spoke! He'd be his normal self on the pitch, ask if I wanted a lift, and when the car doors closed: silence. He would drive, park up, get his dick out and I'd copy.'

'So how did his wife catch you?'

'One night, in the car, out of nowhere he put his hand around my neck. I knew what he wanted.'

I closed my eyes for a second. The image was too good. I'd seen Pricey's car before, pulling into school. It was nothing amazing: a black Audi. But now it shimmered like an Aston Martin in my mind.

'Half-an-hour later I swallowed my first load,' he continued. 'The next time he swallowed mine. Soon I would suck him off as he drove, if it was dark. He would suck me when we stopped. Then more and more clothes started coming off.'

The cogs in my head glided into place.

'Eventually the car got too small,' I said.

'Yup. One Saturday instead of driving to our usual spot he took me to his. He said his wife was out and we had a few hours. Next thing you know we're in his bed and he's telling me to stick my tongue in his arse. You can guess the compromise we came to.'

I suppressed a laugh. *Mr. Price taking it like a champ. Go figure.*

'She came back early, didn't she?' I said.

Nodding his head slowly up and down he said, 'I was pulling on a condom and there was a gasp from behind. She started to say, "you cheating bastard", but when she realised I wasn't him ... She was devastated.

'She kept crying and crying, slumped on the floor in the doorway. Tim pushed me off and went to her but it didn't matter. She slapped and punched and pushed him and he just sat naked next to her taking it. I had to practically step over them both to get out of the house. I can still see her face when I close my eyes.'

I'd seen her before. Once. She'd dropped her husband off by the gates at school. Slender, blonde, big tits she was exactly the kind of woman you'd expect Pricey to be married to. Exactly the kind of woman who would never have seen it coming.

Not that I cared. I only cared about one thing. Myself. Reaching out I put a hand on Adam's leg. He turned and looked at me. His eyes teary.

'It's not your fault,' I said

'Yes, it is. I'm the reason he went crazy, Oscar. I'm the reason he lost his job.'

'The school knows?'

'No, not like that. Fuck knows what would have happened if she'd known I was one of his students.'

'You were sixteen. It's legal. What were they going to do?'

'It's not legal if he's your teacher, Oscar. It's called a position of trust. I looked it up online. He could have gone to jail.'

I said nothing.

'His wife thought I was just some guy. Some faggot he'd picked up.'

I winced. The self-hatred dripping from his lips was undeniable.

Then I realised it was now or never. Turn up the heat or lose him forever to self-pity. I punched him. As hard as I could on the arm.

'What the fuck was that for?!'

'Listen to yourself, mate. You're being ridiculous,' I said.

'Fuck you. No I'm not.'

'Yeah you are. It's not your fault. It's his.'

'It isn't. He didn't force himself on me. I chose to fuck him.'

'And so would anyone else in your position. Trust me. Like seriously, *trust me*. You can't beat yourself up over this.'

'What, so you will?' he said, rubbing his arm.

54

'Sorry,' I said, taking his hand away and kissing his shoulder. 'But you need to understand. That, there, is real pain. The pain eating you up inside your head isn't real. It was, when it happened. It must have sucked. But now you need to let go or else you'll miss out on some pretty awesome shit.'

'Like fucking you.'

'Like fucking me,' I said with a wink.

He smiled.

'I feel guilty,' he said.

'Yeah. You're human. You do something shit, you feel bad. But I bet you've never told anyone that before, have you?'

'No.'

'And I bet you feel better now, don't you?'

'No.'

Raising my eyebrows, I tilted my head towards him. Raised my fist. Said, 'Don't make me hit you again.'

He laughed. Said, 'Fine. A little. Why are you being so nice to me?'

Because I need you to fuck me, you idiot.

'Because being nice is easier than being a twat. Sometimes.'

He laughed again and shivered. He was getting cold, naked on his parents' bed. So was I.

'Here,' I said, crawling across and sliding under the sheets. 'Get in.'

Without a word, he pulled back the covers and twisted himself under. Facing me so his nose almost touched mine. For a while we looked at each other, saying nothing. The smell of fresh linen filling our nostrils and the gentle buzz of the light switch the only sound.

Turning I shuffled my body against his. He put his arm over me and we spooned.

The sun was shining when we woke, and I couldn't have been happier that I'd waited to catch that monkey.

Six

It hadn't been my intention to stay, even when I'd knocked on Adam's door to find him standing like my dreams wrapped in muscle.

Sleepovers weren't my style. Leaving cut out the bullshit that came after whoever I was with was done. The fake affection. The forced interest. The meaningless questions.

They didn't care. They didn't really give a toss about my life. I was a distraction to them. A plaything out of who knows how many other toys they could have picked from a digital shelf. That's what they were to me so what's the point?

With Adam, however, there was a point. A big one.

Not because, somewhere over the course of our thoroughly enjoyable evening, I'd had a change of heart. It took finding myself stranded on the other side of the planet to have that, many years later. No, curling up beside him that Saturday night was tactical, pure and simple.

Yes, I was high. Yes, I'll admit, it was nice lying in his arms and feeling his powerful chest rise and fall behind me. To say it wasn't soothing would be a lie.

But I'd had no idea about Pricey. Mr. Tim Price sexiest man alive. None. And when Adam had told me his story, in all its cock-hardening glory, an idea had sprung to life between my attentive ears.

I'd stayed the night because I needed to make him trust me. And I'd known, when morning would come, he wouldn't be able to control himself. He would have gone from wanting me, to needing me.

I wasn't wrong.

'You awake?' he whispered in my ear.

My eyes were closed but I could feel his elbow sinking the mattress and propping up his head behind me. His body was close but not touching. I could feel his heat.

Laying still I kept my breath slow and controlled, adding a subtle snore here and there for good measure.

He has to try harder than that.

Slowly lowering himself he changed tactics.

His cock came first. Hard and thick he pushed himself into me. His shaft between my arse cheeks and the head against the small of my back.

His pecs came next. Large and firm they pressed into my shoulder blades before his fatless abdomen followed. Under the covers a hand found my waist and gently took hold. His forehead nestled into my hair. His breath heated my neck.

That's better.

Letting out a yawn I stretched against him. Then, arching my back, I pushed my arse until I could feel the blood pumping through his cock against my hole. His grip on my waist tightened and I opened my eyes.

Looking at me through pale morning light was myself. My head on a plush white pillow I didn't recognise. A tuft of my short brown hair jutting out of place. The shape of a huge body I barely knew, but would recognise anywhere, behind me.

A devious smile crept over my face. The body began to grind.

Slowly at first. Then harder when I reached my hands behind my head and around his neck. My biceps bulging back at me in the mirror as I linked my fingers together.

Gliding a hand over my abs he pulled me into him as close as possible. Effortlessly. I was taller than most lads in my year and built from years of swimming, but I was as light as a feather in his arms.

Letting go of his neck I twisted my upper body and found his lips. Fast and hungry we tasted each other; neither of us bothered about the taste and smell of stale beer and tobacco on our breath.

For minutes we got lost in the gentle jostling of our tongues as birds tweeted somewhere outside. My fingers pinching his nipples and digging into his muscles. His holding me tight and pulling my arse against him over and over.

Then he moved his face away, stuck two fingers in his mouth, sucked them, pulled them out and reached down.

'Whoa,' I said, pulling my arse away from his oncoming reach. 'What do you think you're doing?'

'What?' he said, a look of genuine confusion plastered across his handsome face. 'Don't you want to?'

'Don't ask dumb questions,' I said, a cheeky smile spreading across mine.

'Then what?'

I nodded my head at the mirror. Said, 'Where's the rush?'

Looking up he caught his own reflection. Smiled.

'No rush,' he said.

'Good.'

'Where shall we start?'

Throwing off the sheet I laid on my stomach. Raising my arse into the air I turned my head ninety degrees and looked back at the mirror.

I could see us both. My naked profile from head to toes. Him kneeling next to me. Staring. His cock jutting out from his body like a spear.

'Hungry?' I said.

Smirking he raised his hand slowly and placed it on the back of my thigh. He clasped tight. Squeezed my muscle. Then he let go and slid his grip up and over my arse cheeks.

Slap.

He spanked me hard. Pain, quickly followed by pleasure, burned over my skin as air hissed through my teeth and into my lungs.

'You like that?' he said.

Slap. Again, before I could answer.

'You know I do,' I said, now relishing the hot prickle of his hand across my reddening left cheek; my eyes fixed on the polished glass.

'Good,' he said, swinging a knee over me.

Squeezing his legs, he pushed mine together until they touched. Then, pulling my cheeks apart with both hands, he held me open and took in the view. I didn't need the mirror to know my arse still looked great. Pert, tight, smooth, hairless.

Nothing's changed since last night.

He licked his lips. Satisfied, his back curved upwards and his mouth lowered onto me.

All around him the strengthening sunlight poured into the room, reflecting against lint and dust in the air. Rays of white shone around his body as his mouth unhurriedly ate. He knew what he was doing this time.

Heaven.

Seconds morphed into minutes. My breath growing heavier and his tongue pushing deeper. Blood rushed to my face and tiny salty droplets formed on my forehead. My cock aching beneath me, stuck between my surging body and the mattress.

Burying my face in the pillow my mind raced. Images of him flashed across the darkness like a movie as my hole got hotter and wetter. Every fibre of my body wanted to feel how rough this rugby captain could play. How powerful he could be. I wanted him to unleash everything he had.

Destroy me.

Turning back to the reflection I reached behind and pulled his head away from my hole by his hair. Hot turned to cold as his lips smacked away from their feast.

'What?' he said.

'Finger me.'

'Yeah?'

'Yeah.'

Without hesitating he drove two thick fingers inside me to the knuckle. Index and middle.

A wave of intensity rolled up my spine, through my gut and stomach and into my throat. There it became a moan of pleasure unapologetically resounding through the morning stillness like a call to prayer. Pushing my upper body off the bed and locking my arms, I let gravity pull me down even deeper. Then, pushing my arse against his grinding hand, I lifted myself by my knees and assumed the position.

Woof.

Back and forth I rocked myself, harder and deeper. Turning and twisting his hand in time, his fingers curled

and wound inside me. His muscles bugling beautifully as
his huge arm pistoned like a well-oiled machine.

But the view. *It's not good enough.*

'Turn me,' I said.

'What?'

He didn't like being interrupted.

'Turn me so I can see.'

Luckily he was easily persuaded.

Pulling out and grabbing my hips with both hands,
he yanked me. My hole gaped open for a split-second
before the fabric below blurred and I flew down the bed,
weightless and submissive.

Hopping off the bed he stood and turned my body
so I was diagonal. I could see it all. My slim, tensed back,
my arse, my cheeks, my pink hole in the air. Him.

Everything is perfect. Nothing can go wrong.

'I'm ready,' I said.

'Me too.'

'Go get the condoms.'

He froze. Momentarily, but it was certainly a latex
spanner in his works. The look on his face when I'd
mentioned protection the night before had told me
everything I'd needed to know.

Why use a rubber when they're on the pill, right?

'Come on,' he said, stroking my arse.

'Sorry mate.'

Three.

'Why not?'

''Cos I said so.'

Two.

'I'll pull out.'

'Nope.'

One.

'Please?'

Direct hit.

There, in his parents' bedroom, Adam Stanmore, school hero, Mr. Number One, begging me, the social nobody, the gay boy, the faggot.

For three whole seconds I was silent, basking in the triumph sweeping over me. I wanted to shout and yell and laugh hysterically.

I won.

Then all I had to do was grab my stuff, get changed and leave. Leave him hanging. Leave him wanting more. He'd be the Puppet King but I'd be the hand pulling the strings.

But I couldn't. He spat in his hand and began to rub his cock. Slowly. Seductively. Each stroke leaving a layer of lubrication glistening in the sunlight.

My poker face was flawless but he knew I was suddenly sucking down saliva faster. He knew I wanted it. And I did.

Bad.

Jumping my knees forward I turned and kneeled on the bed, facing him. Taking hold of his cock, I leant forward and ran my tongue from base to tip. Kissed up his pre-cum.

'I suppose I have already swallowed your load,' I said.

He grinned.

'And I suppose you've never taken one in your arse, right?'

'A load?'

I nodded.

'Nope. Never.'

'Ever been tested?' I said.

'Yup. All clear. You?'

'Same.'

And I wasn't lying.

'Ok,' I said, resuming my position.

He grinned. Like an ape.

'Where should I cum?' he said.

Looking over my shoulder, I stared into his eyes. He was waiting. Waiting for me.

'Wherever you want,' I said.

As I'd come to expect, he started slow. Careful and courteous.

A long, thick strand of foamy white fell from his mouth. I watched it drop and heard its tiny clap against his cock. He shifted his weight and the bed compressed. Then a strong hand on the base of my back pushed down, lifting my arse up higher.

I watched the head of his cock rest between my cheeks and felt it gooey against my hole, every detail gleaming back at us from the polished glass of his parents' mirror. I saw his arse tense and knew that was my cue to relax my own as best I could.

Millimetre by millimetre he stretched me open further than I'd ever been opened before. One inch, two inches, three inches, four. Reaching behind I put my hand on the base of his abs.

'Easy does it,' I said.

Taking a deep lungful, I tried to focus on my breath. Then, moving my hand away slowly, he continued. Five inches, six inches, seven. He hit my prostate and froze.

'What's that?' he said, panic in his voice.

I tried to answer but I was too busy trying to breathe.

'Is that?' he said, eyes wide.

64

I composed myself.

'No. It's my prostate. Girls don't have them.'

'Oh,' he said, relief flooding his face as he pushed himself against it again. 'Does it hurt?'

'Fuck no,' I moaned. 'It's amazing.'

'Awesome,' he said, sliding in his final three inches.

My hole clamped around him as my brain, unable to stop my neck and head from whipping back, flooded my body with dopamine. He groaned, highest volume, holding his position. His deep voice reverberating through his body and into mine. My cock on the verge of exploding.

'Wow,' he said, sliding out to the tip, pushing all the way in again and pulling back out completely. 'Nobody's ever been able to take it all.'

Pushing myself off the mattress I arched my back to vertical and held onto his neck. Twisting my chest, I pulled his head down and bit his lip.

Stupid boy.

Seven

They say time stands still during important moments in our lives.

First kisses. First loves. Births. Deaths. And you'll always remember what you were doing when you heard about so and so, or where you were when this or that happened.

But time doesn't stand still. It can't. The universe doesn't work that way, at least not for us. What happens is, in these moments, our concept of beginning, middle and end goes completely out the metaphorical window because how long doesn't matter.

All that matters is the present. The now. For however as long as your brain needs to latch itself back onto reality.

That Sunday morning was one. Because Adam was alive. Alive with energy. Alive with desire. And, most importantly, alive with freedom.

With all that fuelling muscles trained to scrum and blood prepared to pump faster and harder than men twice his age, he didn't let my brain keep track of time.

It couldn't.

All it could process was my senses, surging and sparking from the rapid pulse of his thrusts. Each spit-lubricated pump rippling shockwaves of pleasure, ablaze with beautiful pain, through my entirety.

I'd wanted to see how strong he could be and he displayed his power mercilessly.

My cock, rock hard and ready to blow, slapped against my stomach. My knees and arms and legs and back were braced and flexed and arched for maximum comfort and depth.

My neck and shoulders glistened with sweat, squeezed out from almost every pore. My head was hot and wetter. Dancing by itself to a rhythm drummed from behind.

Every part of me wanted more. Every electrified cell whirred and purred as I submitted, taking what I was given. My breath was fast and deep. His breath the same. My moans were loud. His were louder.

Fabric squeaked between my teeth and bed slats creaked. The headboard beat incessantly against the wall. The smell of two teenage boys in an adult's room filled our nostrils and the glorious sight of us was reflected into our open, hungry eyes at all times.

I watched his muscles bulge and tense. His hands clamp, strong and commanding. His hips lunge back and forth. His neck, his shoulders, his back, his arse. His cock. Me.

We could have fucked for hours. Or minutes. I have no idea. It was a living dream.

Until he was about to cum. That I remember with picture-perfect clarity. When his breath was heaviest, his thrusts hit hardest and his grip held tightest. When, panting from exhaustion, he said some of my favourite words in all the English language.

'I'm going to blow.'

I tried to reply but my words weren't working. Instead my load stirred inside my balls as his heavy hanging sack slapped against me. Two large droplets of sweat dripped from his forehead onto my back.

'I'm going to blow!' he said again.

I didn't even bother attempting to talk. Instead I grabbed myself and locked my eyes on the mirror.

Just in time.

Sliding all the way out he leaned back on his knees and took hold of himself. My insides shifted and I saw my reddened hole gape open, dark and empty and almost perfectly circular. His body shuddered. Every muscle from his neck to his calves contracted and bulged. His arse clenched. His arm worked as fast as it could.

Thick and white his load shot between my cheeks. I watched it pour into my open hole. Tantalisingly hot over my sensitive, beaten skin. Spurt by spurt it seeped inside me.

My turn.

Tightening my grip, I lifted my arse higher and stretched my knees further apart. The veins in my cock pressed against my palm. His load travelled onwards.

'Push it in,' I said.

Without a word, he did. Filled me a final time as a bead of sweat ran down my face and I blew.

My load was big. It streaked across the bed, leaving a gooey white line on the sheets from my belly button to my neck. More and more poured out, over my hand and dripping between my fingers, as he slowly and steadily churned his own. His legs jolting as my hole tightened around him.

Unable to take anymore he pulled out. Then he swung himself off the bed and stood up slowly.

Collapsing onto the mattress and into my wet patch, I looked up at him. For a minute neither of us spoke a

68

word. We simply stared at each other. Panting and sweating.

I relished every detail. He loomed over me. Like a giant.

'You enjoy that?' I said.

'You have no idea.'

Throwing himself onto the bed he landed next to me, bouncing me an inch. Then, grabbing me in his arms, he rolled on top, his sweaty six-pack gliding over mine.

Here it comes. Pillow talk.

'You're seriously sexy, Oscar.'

'I know,' I said.

He laughed.

'Mind if I shower?' I said.

'Huh?'

I repeated my question.

'Shit, sorry,' he said, releasing me from his hold and shuffling back to his side of the bed.

Pointing to the landing he said, 'Second on the left. Want me to show you where the towels are?'

'I'm sure I'll manage.'

Ten minutes later I found him where I'd left him. Spread-eagled and naked on the bed. His cock soft but still huge. He looked up and opened his arms expectantly. He wanted to cuddle.

I wanted to laugh in his face.

But I couldn't. There was one more thing I needed. One last piece of vital information.

Smiling I took off the towel from around my waist and bypassed his intimacy by straddling him. Putting his hands behind his head he relaxed and beamed up at me. I tickled his chin.

I have to do this right.

'I know this is random, but I was thinking about what you told me. About Mr. Price,' I said.

'Oh yeah?'

'Yeah. How do you know?' I said.

'Know what?'

'That it was your fault.'

His brow wrinkled.

'I mean, I know it's a stretch, but there could be another reason why he went mental.'

He shook his head and looked to the side. Said, 'No. I know it was me.'

'How?'

'He told me.'

'You're still in touch?' I said nonchalantly.

'No, not like that. I bumped into him.'

'Sure. You "bumped" into him,' I said, squeezing his nipple between my thumb and index finger.

'Fuck off,' he said, play punching my arm.

I dodged his blow. Said, 'I'm not wrong though, am I?'

'Ok. I went to his house.'

I pulled a face. A face that said "poor you". A face that hid my desired reaction.

'He lives local then?' I said.

'Yeah. Not far from here. But he wasn't home. So I went to the old creek field. He goes running there some evenings. I just wanted to see him, you know? But he wouldn't even look me in the eye.'

And like that, I had everything I needed.

'Do you think he'll ever talk to me again?' he said.

I'm not proud of what happened next. How I treated him. All he'd wanted was someone to talk to. Someone he could confide in. Someone who would listen. But that

70

Oscar, the one sitting on the lap of Adam Stanmore, wasn't ready to forgive.

'Hey?' Adam said.

I ignored him. Didn't even look him in the eye. I jumped off his lap, turned and walked. Out of the room, down the hall and into his bedroom. I was already half dressed by the time he poked his head around the door, sheepish and confused.

'What are you doing?' he said.

I said nothing. Didn't look up.

'Cool, cool. Yeah, it is cold in here. I can turn the heating on if you like? My folks don't get home for ages. We could smoke a spliff. Get sweaty again.'

I said nothing. Didn't look up.

'Are you leaving?'

Nothing.

I felt his confused eyes follow me as I scooped up my trainers and walked past him toward the stairs. He reached out and put a gentle hand on my shoulder.

I stopped still, turned my head slowly and looked at his hand.

'You really want me to stay?' I said.

'Of course,' he said. 'Why would you think I'd want you to leave?'

Letting go of my shoulder he bent down and pulled on some underwear.

'We could hang out,' he said.

I sneered at him.

'Like mates?' I said.

His smile wavered. Said, 'Yeah, like mates.'

I looked him up and down. One last time. He really was sexy. Totally my type. Strong, built, fit, tall, handsome.

But fuck me he's stupid.

'No thanks,' I said.

He said nothing. Stared at me with a face that said it all. No one had ever rejected him before. Adam Stanmore. Mr. Perfect.

'Well, this is riveting,' I said, continuing past him and down the stairs.

'Wait,' he said.

Thud, thud, thud went his heavy footsteps after me. 'Wait!'

At the bottom of the staircase I stopped and turned. A few stairs above, he towered over me. I felt like David versus Goliath. The part where he's about to pick up the rock.

'What?' I said.

'I don't get it, man. What did I say?'

'Come on, Adam, really?'

Again, he said nothing. If I could have heard the cogs turning in his head before, now they were practically screeching.

'Yeah, really. Tell me,' he said.

I should have left. Left it there. But the twisted part of me had tasted blood and wanted more. I attacked.

'Ok. You're a hypocrite. And an idiot.'

He flinched, like my words had slapped him across the face. His brow furrowed. Sadness and anger crept into his eyes. His lips drooped into a frown.

Taking the final stairs slowly he sat on the third from bottom with his shoulders slumped. I'd never seen such a big guy look so small before.

'I don't understand,' he said.

'There's a surprise.'

'Fuck you.'

'You just did.'

'Why are you being like this?'

'Mate, I'm being honest.'

'Honest? About what? How am I a hypocrite?'

I was getting impatient. I raised my eyebrows.

'What?!' he yelled.

I shook my head and leaned against the wall.

'You really think I've forgotten?'

'Forgotten what?'

'That morning at school when everyone found out?'

It took him a second. Then he got it. Guilt joined the mix of emotions splattered across his face.

'Yeah. You remember now, don't you?' I said. 'You remember standing there, laughing and joking as they circled me. You remember what they did. How they left me on the ground for the teachers to scrape up. Fucked up and bleeding.'

'I didn't touch you.'

My fists clenched and fury sizzled in my stomach. The urge to punch him in the face and keep on punching caught light and flared in my heart and hands. I wanted him to know how it had felt. I wanted him to feel the pain.

Instead I exhaled. Deeply. Choking the flames to a gentle simmer.

'You're right,' I said. 'You didn't. You didn't do anything. Like everyone else you just stood there and let it happen. But now, guess what? Now I know you were just, if not more of a faggot than me. And you did nothing. You're worse than the rest of them.'

For five seconds, there was silence. A heavy, suffocating silence. Then he said, 'You felt this way all along?'

'Yes.'

'What was last night? This morning? Everything you said was bullshit?'

'I don't even remember what I said. I'm not your friend, Adam.'

'You were using me?'

I cocked my head to the side and smiled.

'Finally. Proof that you're not completely retarded. Yes, I was using you. And how useful you've been.'

'What's that supposed to mean?'

'It means I've got to go. Need to save my energy for my run around the old creek field later.'

Clenching his fists, he stood up and came at me. Squaring my shoulders, I puffed out my chest and met him halfway. He was humongous. Hard and fuming his breath blasted my forehead from flared nostrils. But I stood my ground.

'Go on then. Do your worst,' I said.

'Get out.'

'Gladly,' I said walking to the door.

Holding the cool metal of the handle I turned and took a final look. One last look at the King of School. Defeated.

'Oh,' I said pulling the door open.

Sunlight poured all around me and into the hallway. He lifted his hand to shield his eyes from the rays beaming around my body.

'If you try anything at school,' I said. 'I will ruin you.'

Eight

Adam didn't go in to school the next day.

Or the day after. But when he did, a chilly, autumn Wednesday, he brought a black eye, two broken ribs and one hell of a revelation with him.

'Have you heard about Stanmore?'

'I can't believe it.'

'What?'

'He's a batty boy.'

'Fuck off!'

'Seriously.'

'Yeah, his dad beat the shit out of him for bumming some lad in their house.'

'He's telling people he's bi.'

'What's the difference?'

'I dare you to say that to him.'

'Piss off, he's built like a brick shithouse.'

And so on.

It turned out, after our heart-to-heart that weekend, Adam had gone soul searching. And what he'd found had been too heavy. When his parents had come home, he'd unburdened himself on them.

I don't know what he'd told them. I'm sure he hadn't gone into every minute detail, or maybe he had. But after what his father had done to him, Adam Stanmore had stopped caring about what other people thought.

That's what he told me anyway.

He was waiting for me after the final bell in the staff car park. I always walked home through it. Less kids. More adults keeping an eye out for trouble.

'Oi.'

Looking up from my phone it took me a couple seconds to find him, leaning against the side of the art block in the shadow of a nearby oak tree. For six-foot-six he was good at hiding.

Walking over I said nothing as nearby cars and buses filled the air between us with their daily rumbles.

'I'm sorry about Sunday,' he said.

I put my phone in my trouser pocket. With an opener like that he had my full attention.

'You are? What for?'

'Urm.'

Rolling my eyes, I turned to leave. *He still doesn't get it.*

'Wait,' he said.

I sighed and stopped and locked eyes with him again. The large, dark purple bruise spoiling his flawless face looked sore and a twinge of guilt pricked me in the stomach.

I ignored it. Easily.

'Go on,' I said.

'I'm sorry I didn't help you when you needed it. That I stood by and let them do that to you.'

I hadn't expected that. In all honesty, I hadn't expected to hear from him again at all. An apology was an interesting turn of events to say the least.

A genuine one too.

I threw my bag down next to his. Books thudded and stationary rattled, joining the din from the road. Walking over to the tree, I leaned against it, facing him.

76

The brittle, cold bark dug into my back through my dark navy-blue blazer and memories of the weekend tugged at my balls as I took him in, face-on.

His bedroom. His parents' bed. The mirror. But I'm still angry.

'So, what? You think telling everyone at school you suck cock makes up for it?' I said.

His battered eyes widened as much as they could. He'd probably expected a different reply. Perhaps he thought I'd be more understanding.

'Kind of,' he said, stroking his arm, just like he'd done when he'd told me about Mr. Price.

'How?' I said.

'Now you're not the only one people know about. Now you're not alone.'

'So?'

'So, it'll be easier for you.'

'And you believe that?'

'Yes.'

'Then you really are an idiot.'

'Why?'

'Look, Adam, I appreciate the apology. Honestly, that was a nice surprise. But just because you didn't make up some rugby injury about your fucked-up face, doesn't stop you from being the rugby captain. They won't treat you like they treat me. You're too much of a paradox.'

His brow wrinkled, as much as it could. With a messed-up mug, he still looked cute when he didn't understand big words.

'What do you mean?' he said.

'I mean you confuse them. They'll talk shit behind your back, and you might lose a few mates. Hey, you might even lose your team, but no one's going to do to you what they did to me. No one will dare. Besides,' I said looking his weakened but still gigantic frame up and down. 'They literally can't.'

He looked at his feet, frowning. Then there was a noise to our side: a shuffle of shoes on concrete. We turned in unison to see a year-seven boy walking around the corner. He froze at the sight of us, fear filling his tiny, young face. He had a cello in a black fabric case on his back. It was bigger than him.

I looked away. Adam leaned into the shadows. The kid walked on.

'My dad tried. To do what they did to you,' Adam said.

Guilt again. Ignored again.

'I heard.'

'He's in hospital.'

'See.'

He said nothing.

'What did you do to him?' I said.

'Shattered his jaw. Fractured his skull.'

'Fuck. How?'

'I don't remember. It was over before I knew what happened.'

A family photo I'd seen in his kitchen flashed across my mind. Mum, Dad and Adam in their finest wedding attire. Mr. Stanmore senior was a big guy, as you'd expect, but not as big as Adam. It would have been clear to anyone junior had the upper hand.

Rage blinds.

'What did he do to you?' I said.

'He punched me. Hard. I think he broke a finger because something cracked and the doctor said it wasn't my eye socket. When I didn't get up he kicked me in the chest. Then the crack was definitely mine.'

I winced. Said, 'Something else we have in common.'

'Your dad?'

'No,' I said, gesturing at the school with my head. 'Broken ribs.'

We said nothing for a few seconds. Both reliving memories we'd rather forget. Adam broke the silence.

'It was when he went for the kitchen knife and mum started screaming that I blacked out. The next thing I know I'm standing over him. My hands are shaking and my knuckles are bleeding. He's unconscious. His face pissing blood.'

I said nothing.

'Mum said she thought I was going to kill him,' he said.

Then neither of us spoke again. He stared at the sports field behind me, only days ago a lush, green playground now pot-holed and muddy and filled with uncertainty in his mind.

I watched a group of teachers make their way to their cars. They looked our way, ready to move us on, but then their faces changed and they stayed quiet, muttering a word or two to each other instead.

'You find Mr. Price then?' he said.

I jumped at his words and fixed narrowed eyes on him as adrenaline gripped my body. My heartbeat quickened and my muscles tensed. But his posture was timid. As timid as it could get. And there was no aggression in his voice. No emotion full stop.

'Not yet,' I said.

'Are you going to?'

I sighed. *Undoubtedly.*

'What I do is my business. Just like what you do is yours,' I said.

'Alright, calm down. I was going to say, if you have, or if you are then go for it. Hopefully he won't fuck up your head too.'

Another interesting turn of events. *Very interesting.*

'You changed your tune,' I said.

'Yeah, it's funny how quickly that can happen. I just don't care anymore.'

'About?'

'Any of it.'

'You and me both,' I said.

He looked at me and smiled.

'What?' I said.

'I was thinking.'

'That's new for you.'

He gently kicked the side of my shoe. Gravel scraped and, in the natural light, his undamaged eye twinkled bright and blue.

'Piss off,' he said.

'I was trying to.'

He laughed but regretted it immediately. Placing a large hand on his chest he took a long, slow breath.

'I was thinking you're right. It is different for you than me,' he said, his voice struggling through pain.

'And?'

'It doesn't have to be.'

It was my turn to laugh.

'What, you're going to set up a pride march?' I said.

'No, but I can watch your back.'

I wanted to laugh again but it didn't come. No one had said that to me before. My inner-cynic momentarily silenced, I pushed myself off the tree and stepped closer.

'You'd do that? After everything I said to you?' I said.

'Maybe not right now,' he said, with a hint of anger in his eyes. 'But when I'm better.'

'Why?'

'I look out for you. You look out for me.'

My laugh managed to make its way out.

'How exactly am I going to look out for you?' I said.

He stepped closer. Didn't even look to see if anyone was coming. Then, placing his huge hands on my waist, he pulled me in.

'We don't have to be mates. You made that clear enough. But we could have a lot of fun together,' he said.

I've said it before and I'll say it again. Boys like logic. Myself included.

The hairs on my neck stood on end as his words dripped into my ear. All kinds of ideas stirring and growing and taking shape behind my eyes.

Amazing, meaningless, string-free sex and protection from the braindead bigots around the school? That's one hell of a proposal.

Letting go of my waist and leaning back into his hiding spot he said, 'Well?'

'Are you saying what I think you're saying?' I said.

He grinned. Said, 'What do you think I'm saying?'

Stepping into the shadow, I ran the back of my finger down the undamaged side of his chest and over the ridges of his thick, strong six-pack. The cotton of his shirt whispered against my skin until I felt the hard, leather of his belt.

'I think you're saying you enjoyed yourself on the weekend,' I said.

'Didn't you?'

'It wasn't awful.'

'Then what do you reckon?'

'I think there's a flaw in your plan.'

'Is there?'

'Yeah. Where?' I said.

'Where what?'

'Where would we have our fun? My house is off limits, and I'm pretty sure yours is too.'

He folded his arms and smirked. A proper smirk. Through the pain.

'That's where you come in. In exchange for my protection you do what you do best,' he said.

'Which is?'

'Find some lads that would be up for it,' he said.

I smiled. Toothy and wide and verging on manic. That was exactly what I was hoping the big, beat-up idiot would say. Leaning back against my tree, I pulled out my phone and scrolled through recent messages.

Three potentials.

'I don't know. It won't be easy,' I lied.

'That's ok,' he said leaning over slowly and picking up his bag.

Wincing at the pain he kept his stare fixed on something behind me. Turning I saw it: a silver BMW pulling into the parking lot, its shiny black tires crunching over gravel. A worried middle-aged woman was clutching the steering wheel like it was about to roll away.

'I'll be out of action for a couple of weeks at least. You've got plenty of time,' Adam said.

I watched him hobble away slowly. Pained. Bruised. Beaten. Adam Stanmore but different.

'I'll think about it,' I said loud enough for him to hear.

Opening the passenger door, he slid himself into the seat. The woman said something to him but he ignored her. He didn't take his eyes off me until the car started its three-point turn out of the lot.

Picking up my bag, I began my journey home. The long way.

I had a lot to think about.

Nine

It was the third time that week I'd taken the long way home, and like the previous two evenings, it wasn't a decision I'd made lightly.

Walking home was never fun. I didn't look forward to the end of the day. Each time the final bell pierced the silence of the classroom, I knew, in ten minutes, I'd be fair game, and when its shrill, metallic cry rang in my ears I knew that there'd no longer be anyone at least contractually obliged to protect me.

All I could ever do was hang around until they streamed out, pushing and shoving in their laughing packs, and wait for whichever bored, indifferent teacher to give me the look. The look that said, "for the love of god leave".

Then it was always the same. Headphones in, but music off so I could pretend not to hear the oh-so-original and hilarious insults hurled at me from a distance without being deaf to footsteps racing up from behind.

Head down, no eye contact. All the way home.

But this week, even though the longer it took the more chances bored kids had to break more of my bones without fear of suspensions or expulsions, every extra step was worth it.

Since I knew where I could spot his car or catch a glimpse of a shaved head attached to broad, muscular shoulders or those powerful, hairy legs, it was a risk I was willing to take.

Until I find him a three-mile detour around the old creek field is the only way home.

That day, however, the atmosphere along the cold, grey concrete in the early evening dim was different. Lads walked by in their usual groups but talked in hushed voices. I felt their eyes on me as we passed on narrow pavements. Them on their way to the town centre, me the outer suburbs.

But that, as they say, was that.

No names, no shoving. No laughter. By then surely everyone had heard the news. We like to think girls are the gossips, but scratch away macho façades and you'll find it's a human trait indiscriminate of gender. Boys love to bitch. But, their renewed sense of indignation I'd assumed would be waiting for me, was nowhere to be seen or heard.

Another group passed. Quiet. Nothing.

I smiled. After I'd been outed, like Adam I'd given up caring what people had thought or said about me. Caring didn't change anything. But this was interesting.

What it meant, I didn't know, but every step on my journey home somehow felt safer already.

And what a journey. I didn't expect that in a million years.

Adam had apologised. He'd stood there, face to face, and apologised. And then his proposal had been nothing short of genius. For him, at least.

Why stop at two when there are plenty of willing boys?

As the steady flow of headlights trundled by on the road, yellow or white toward, red away, I thought about the others.

I wondered, as the pedestrian crossing beeped overhead and exhaust fumes mingled with the steam from my breath, if they'd be up for it. Up for more than late-night MSN jerk off sessions and brief, clandestine meetings now the King had given his royal decree.

Pulling out my phone and making it incident-free past a group of chavs smoking weed and revving their mopeds by the entrance to a muddy, gravel footpath, I thumbed through my messages. My black shoes crunching onwards and the sweet, sticky second-hand smoke dancing up my nostrils.

There was Daniel. Eighteen. An inch shorter than my six foot, he was toned and muscular from years of playing football. Calves you could sink your teeth into. Amazing arse. Smart too.

Oxbridge-bound, he'd known how it had had to work. Once he'd realised I would never say a word, he'd sent all sorts. First a picture. A grainy image of an eight-inch cock in some girl's mouth. He'd wanted to know if it turned me on.

It hadn't taken much to get him to send more. First more pictures in better quality and more body. Then videos. Girls again followed by solo performances. Then his parents had gone out one night.

Stopping in my tracks, I pressed play on my phone screen. It was only a grainy, nine-second clip but his cock looked amazing sliding in and out of my mouth, and the amplified sound of my saliva sloshing through my earbuds made my own cock blissfully shudder.

The slurping ended and fast feet hitting small stones took its place. They were right behind me but I knew the muffled sound of running trainers. I didn't look up as a jogger shot past in my peripheral in a flash of red. Shuffling my trousers I did the best to hide the lump in my pants and walked on.

Not far now.

Next on the list was James. Five-foot-five he was the perfect teenage pocket bottom. Bright red hair, smooth porcelain skin and the tightest, pertest arse imaginable.

I'd caught him looking at my cock in the library toilets one Friday afternoon a few weeks back.

Naturally the kid had been shy. I didn't blame him for keeping schtum about his sexuality, what with already being ginger and basically a midget, but I'd seen the fire in his eyes. The burning intrigue as he'd looked at me, pleading to be taken into the cubicle and fucked senseless.

Logistics-wise that would have been impossible so I'd fingered him and gotten his number. He would need more practice, being a virgin, if he was going to take Adam and me, but there was no doubt he'd look superb getting stretched open from both ends.

And then there was Phil. Phil was a cum-swallower, not a cock-sucker. Taking dicks in the mouth wasn't his bag, apparently, but slurping down big white mouthfuls was.

Not that I cared. Watching him twitch as my load hit the back of his throat and gushed into his stomach, kneeling in his parent's living room and looking up at me with those big green eyes, made up for any ambiguity. And I was certain he would be keen for two feedings.

The ground underneath turned soft and I looked up from the glare of my phone. A large green field stretched in front, bordered on the far side by the dried-up remains of a thin, bush-lined creek and a medium-sized forest still leafy but beginning to shed its summer coat.

Above it, the weak sun was not far from setting below the tops of the trees and, in the crisp twilight, everything was bathed in an orangey-pink glow. Putting my phone in my pocket I took a seat on a nearby bench.

Quiet today.

A hundred-or-so foot to the right, a middle-aged woman in an oversized, bright blue puffer jacket threw a stick to a long-haired cocker spaniel. It bounded after its prize only to stop disappointed at the feeble distance it had travelled. Lying next to it, it gnawed on the wood and ignored its owner's pleas to return.

Twenty feet behind, a man and woman in scarfs and hats strolled away holding hands. I could see from the pink leads draped around the man's shoulders they were also dog walkers. In the distance two chocolate Labradors bounded and played together, directionless and free.

Lucky bitches.

To the left, a small group of young kids played football. Further on, adults sipped steaming drinks from flasks, talking amongst themselves and keeping at least one eye on the little ones. I assumed Mr. Price didn't have any children, what with being a closet case, but you can't be too sure. I scanned the fathers.

No shaved heads. No rugged physiques. All I found were wrinkled, tired faces and bodies let go under nice clothes picked out by dutiful wives.

Oh the joys of parenthood and marriage.

Standing I took one last look. Left to right. Right to left. No one new. No one else. Another disappointing night. Another pointless detour.

Pulling out my phone I slumped onto the bench. At least I wasn't at a complete loss. Opening a blank message, I typed:

Hey man. I have a proposition for you. When's good to talk?

Then I copied the text and sent identical messages to Daniel, James and Phil. Sitting, I enjoyed the last few minutes of sunlight as the cold wind bit at my neck and hands and face.

I wondered what people did before mobile phones and the internet had been invented. I thought about all the special codes and clothes men had to know and wear if they'd wanted to advertise their status without being thrown in jail or beaten or worse.

Then I made a bet with myself that James would be the first to reply. Daniel's fondness for multimedia worked in his favour, but James was eager. He'd never failed to text back.

Not that any of them were a for-sure win. *It's anyone's game.*

No more than five minutes had passed when my phone vibrated in my pocket but, as I reached in, a pinprick of red popped into my peripheral. The jogger in the red t-shirt had reappeared, tiny on the horizon. Fixing my gaze I watched him grow, running closer and closer.

No way.

Broad shoulders. Shaved head. Those legs. I recognised them anywhere.

I'd stared at them enough, dreaming of running my tongue up the inside of each thigh and tasting his sweat. Feeling their heat locked around my head.

Grabbing my bag, I pulled out my sweater and a book. Plain black. *The Monk.* Then I undid my school tie and bundled it away with my blazer.

He can't see me in my uniform.

I doubted he would remember me: I'd avoided sports like the plague. But after what had happened between him and Adam, it was impossible to know how he would react to another school boy with hunger in his eyes.

Besides, this was a reconnaissance mission, through and through. I needed to confirm his location. That's it. Then, another day, I would launch an attack. How and when I wasn't sure, but then and there, all I could do was throw him a smile or a cheeky wink if he looked my way.

No more.

Placing my bag under the bench I shuffled my feet in front of it, hunched forward, tensed my biceps and opened my book. I was just a young guy, reading in the park after work. Nothing unusual about that.

I looked up, casually, and my heart skipped a beat.

He looks sensational.

No more than twenty metres from me, he had slowed to a walk. His red t-shirt clung to his wide, bulky but toned torso, wet with sweat. Clouds of steam billowed out of his mouth, hanging open and panting for air. His muscular arms bulged with thick, succulent veins and his large hands rested on his waist.

His heavenly legs stamped, step by step, closer and closer, tired but still powerful. His giant, hairy quads stretching the rough, black fabric of his tiny rugby shorts. Haloed by the setting sun behind him every inch of his body looked more amazing than I could remember.

He stopped five metres from me and stretched.

Bending forward he grabbed his ankles and held the position. For a big bloke, he was flexible. Three seconds turned into five. Eight turned to ten. Then he stood up straight, slowly, twisted left and twisted right, reached into the air, stood on tip toes and then stood back down and swung his arms down and around. Then he locked his eyes on me.

I smiled. I winked.

No reaction.

Or if there was, some subtle sign of recognition or excitement or anything at all, he was too far away to tell. He just looked away, passed slowly and continued his jog back down the gravel and away from the field.

Fucking tease.

Pulling my bag from under the bench I stood up and flung it over my shoulder. Watched his bubble arse rise and fall as he ran. Mission successful.

My phone vibrated in my pocket again. New Message from Ginger James.

Mission successful indeed.

Ten

I didn't open James's text for at least another minute.

Maybe two. I was busy being mesmerised.

Mesmerised by the sight in front of me, growing smaller and smaller. Mesmerised by his muscled body, wrapped in a sweaty red t-shirt, and his powerful, beautiful legs pushing further and further along the towering-oak-lined pathway.

I found him.

Before he was a fantasy. He was fiction. When Adam had told me his secret, a part of me had thought it was too good to be true. I didn't think I was out of Mr. Price's league: that hadn't crossed my mind. I was too busy savouring the saltiness of the rugby captain's load on my tongue and between my teeth to think about the coach's.

And even when I'd got it out of him, butt naked and under me, that the coach still lived close, deep down that same part of me still didn't truly believe. I'd decided to go looking, sure, but I wasn't naïve. I hadn't thought it would be easy.

But, four days later in the old creek field, I couldn't believe my luck. He was no longer Mr. Price. He was Tim, six-foot-three and fair game.

For a split-second, I considered following him. Hitching my schoolbag high and chasing him down in my shirt and black trousers. But I wasn't dressed for running.

I had no choice but to stick to my plan and be patient. Something I've always struggled with. Fortunately, I had a five-foot-nothing ginger boy waiting to be played with.

He will keep me nicely occupied.

Pulling out my phone I caught a reflection of myself in the empty screen, lit by the last of the dying sunlight. I was smiling.

Big time.

To get to my house from the field was easy. All I had to do was cut diagonally across, jump the fence and then it was a four-minute home stretch. Thumbing buttons and walking I opened James's reply:

Hey sexy. Sounds interesting! You can come over tonight if you want?

No surprise there. I replied:

Would your parents be cool with me fucking you senseless?

Fifteen steps across the grass and his reply pinged through my headphones, vibrating in my hand.

LOL. Definitely not! I thought you wanted to talk?

I want to do both.

Seven more steps.

Hehe they'll be picking my brother up from judo later. We'll have an hour to ourselves?

I reached the other side of the park and my phone chirped for attention. It was getting dark, quick, and the glow from my screen obscured my vision. I stopped to reply. Falling into the old creek, dried out or not, wasn't on my agenda.

What time?

About 7.

Have you done what I told you? I want your hole smooth.

It took him a little longer to get back to me, but when he did I had to stop again. Not because I couldn't see where I was going. I was already over the fence, back on concrete and under street lamps. But because it was a picture message and deserved my full attention.

Very nice.

I checked the time. Almost six. Replied:

Good boy. Make sure you do the other thing too. See you in an hour.

I wanted to skip the final few hundred yards home, but for obvious reasons I let my thoughts frolic instead. Today was turning out to be one of the best days I'd had in a long time. First Adam. Then Mr. Price. Now James looking better than ever. Even the imminent inevitability of walking through the front door didn't kill my growing erection.

94

It's not that I lived in a particularly bad part of town. It was fine: your bog-standard English patch of grey semidetached houses, all with a small front garden and a bigger, fenced or hedged one out back. Mass built, mundane, unremarkable.

My house was at the end of a street of thirty semidetached boxes, backing onto large, flat fields. The same fields that bordered the town, including behind the old creek field. There were no chavs or drunks hanging about the street corners. People kept to their business. No one stood out.

It was fine. It was what was inside that wasn't.

He didn't hate me for being gay. He didn't beat me like Adam's did. He didn't know. But even if he did he wouldn't have cared. My dad didn't care about anything. Not anymore.

Not since she left.

When I was fifteen I'd come home from school early to find them arguing in the kitchen, and, as usual, they hadn't heard me come in. But something had been different. I'd felt it in the air.

I had looked through the crack in the door. Could only see her, hunched over the table with her head in her hands; her long blond hair cascading over her knuckles and piling in messy heaps around her. Without looking up she'd said she couldn't take anymore. She'd told the tablecloth that now I was old enough, she was getting as far away from this "piece of shit town" as possible.

She'd threatened to leave before. Many times. But there'd been something in her voice that evening. No fury or indignation or desperation. Just emptiness.

She had tucked me in that night for the first time since I was a child. Kissed me on the cheek. Didn't say a word. Gone the next day.

After she'd left, he'd become a shadow of his former self. And he'd already been spineless. He hadn't broken down or gone berserk. He'd switched off: work his dead-end job, sit at his computer, sleep and repeat.

Both their parents had died before I was born so there had been no concerned grandparents to swoop in. Dad had stopped answering his phone. Cut out his friends. He'd gone to the doctor once and came back with a diagnosis of severe depression. Instead of taking his medication, or going to his appointments, he'd done nothing.

One time I'd come home from school to find him hunched over the kitchen table. Like Mum, but with vomit in the sink. He'd told me he didn't want to look at me. According to my drooling, stinking, red-eyed excuse for a father, I reminded him of "her" and that "bitch deserved to die".

We stopped talking after that. Unless you count him throwing his wallet and barking shopping lists at me. Birthdays were forgotten. Christmases too. He hadn't even asked what had happened when I'd come home from school bloodied and beaten and broken one day.

I hated him. I hated them both. Him for never leaving and her for not taking me with her. But at least, in a fucked-up way, they gave me something in return.

Freedom. The freedom to do whatever I wanted, with whoever I wanted. And naturally, at eighteen, I took advantage of every moment.

Warm stale air hit my nostrils as I turned my key and pushed open the front door. It was his signature stench. The kind of smell that told me, once again, he hadn't left the house. Coffee, body odour, human gas, microwave meals.

Kicking off my shoes, I took the stairs two at a time. Didn't have long. Throwing my bag into my room I grabbed a clean towel from the pile of laundry I'd done the night before and made my way down the landing to the bathroom.

As usual Dad's bedroom door was closed as I passed. Only a thin strip of artificial light shone through the gap at the bottom between the carpet and the wood. But I knew he was in. I could hear the machine gun fire of his games and the tap-tap-tap of his keyboard.

Fifteen minutes later I was showered and dressed. Jeans, white briefs, tight white t-shirt and a navy sweater, also nicely tight around my torso. I did my hair and brushed my teeth and looked myself up and down in the mist-bordered bathroom mirror.

Not bad at all.

Back in my room I pulled on my trainers, grabbed my wallet and phone and another two minutes later I was back on the street, waiting for the bus to take me into town. It arrived a minute late.

My fare paid, I took a seat. I had two miles, five stops and plenty of time to check on progress.

On the bus. Won't be long. You ready?

Almost. It took longer than expected. Just getting dressed. My parents probably thought I was wanking in there.

Would you prefer they knew what you were actually doing?

Good point. Ready now. Do you have condoms?

A couple.

Cool. I have some too. And lube.

You ARE a good boy.

Hehe thanks. You remember the address, right?

Scrolling through his previous messages I found what I was looking for.

Yup. I'm almost at your stop.

Can't wait xx

Rolling my eyes, I put my phone in my pocket. Kisses on the end of messages made me cringe. Like this kid thought there was more to our relationship, as if I'd bought him flowers or asked him out for dinner.

I fingered him in a toilet for fuck's sake.

Making a mental note to ensure everything was crystal clear by the end of the night, I pushed the red stop button on the metal pole next to me. As the metallic chime rang out, I hauled myself to the front of the bus. The huge mechanical box slowed to a stop and the door hissed open.

Thanking the driver, I hopped onto the pavement and into the cold evening air. I hadn't been to James's before, but we'd spoken about me coming over plenty of times. About what I'd do to him.

98

I looked around in the darkness. There was no doubt in my mind: James lived in the good part of town.

Not that there was much to see at first. Stretching left to right and around as the road curved out of view wasn't an array of huge houses, rising tall and looking down at the street and the ants below. They were further back, away from the public footpath.

Instead stood a tall, continuous brick wall, open intermittently to make room for all manner of security gates or wide gravel driveways.

A few steps from the bus stop was a large set of spiked, black metal gates two foot taller than my six. To the right of the impressive barricade was a small intercom screen and a double-digit number in a plain, unassuming font. Seventy-three.

I checked my phone again. When he'd said his drive was right by the bus stop he'd meant it was literally next to it. I thumbed a quick message, to tell him I was here, but before I hit send the gates began to open. Taking a step back I enjoyed the theatrics.

The mechanism creaked and groaned and then whirred loudly as the spiked metal barriers jutted open. Then the grumble of a powerful, approaching car filled the air before a black Mercedes poked its nose out of the drive. It was too dark to see the driver. The car pulled out and I watched its red lights blaze in the darkness as it cruised away.

I was already through the gates and halfway up the drive before I heard the mechanism lurch back into action behind me, my sights set solely in front.

This is some place.

Illuminated by subtle outdoor up-lighting was a three-storey Edwardian manor house with elegant, grid windows and two symmetrical front-facing dormers.

It loomed ever closer as I took step after step on the gravel; first hard and compressed from countless car wheels and then crunchier and unstable as I reached the bright red front door. The knocker was heavy. It boomed like a drum. Three times.

Silence.

I knocked again. Twice. Then I heard swift footsteps running down a flight of stairs inside. They reached ground level. The handle creaked as it turned but the door pulled inwards almost silently.

Dwarfed by his impressive surrounds stood James. His short, thick hair glowing orange next to the red door. His bright blue eyes, filling first with surprise, then excitement, looked straight into mine. His freckled face brightened as he smiled a full, white set of flawless teeth.

Around his torso was a tight, emerald green t-shirt. He was skinny but undeniably more toned out of his baggy school uniform. His legs were bare, apart from a pair of tight, white briefs.

Then they were wrapped around my waist.

Eleven

It was like he jumped into my arms in slow motion.

First, I watched his eyes. Big and blue. Bluer under his thick, ginger locks. They locked onto mine as he leant against the door. Behind him a bright foyer opened into a chandelier-lit great room. His stare suited the place.

It dazzled.

But not like the architecture did. That dazzled in a different way. It was old and impressive. His eyes radiated excitement and youth. Mischief.

Then they changed. In a flash. Something deep-set and primal flickered across their glistening surfaces. It took hold and erupted out and over the rest of his body.

It curled the corners of his smile. It lowered his head and neck and shoulders. It rippled through his chest and pulled his hold from the door. It bent his knees. It compressed him like a spring. Then it told his legs to push and pounce.

I didn't blink. I watched every second as my muscles braced and my arms came up to catch him. My mouth opening like his.

Snapshots of our first meeting in the library toilets at school flashed through my head: his lightly freckled hands flat against the cold, white-washed brick. The inside of his cotton underwear against the back of my hand. The sweet smell of his hair wax and the salty taste of his neck.

Blood rushed to my cock as the memory of his tight, spit-lubed hole warmed my right middle finger. Some of the first words he'd ever said to me, fast and whispered between quick, sharp breaths, echoed in my mind as we connected like a pair of highly-charged magnets.

"Please fuck me".

His mouth was hot and his tongue was wild against my own. It flicked and danced inside my mouth, matching the hunger that had commanded his body moments before. His breath was fast and feverish, punctuated with gasps and boyish giggles.

The tops of his porcelain white arms, bulging with mini biceps, warmed my cheeks. His hands played with my hair. His arse fit perfectly inside my palms. I could have held him up for hours.

My cock ached and pulled my underwear tight under my jeans as thoughts of bending his small frame like a pretzel tried to control me. I yearned to watch his blushing face wince as I took his virginity.

But first we needed to move out of the doorway. We had an hour, and, by the two or so seconds I'd had to glance around the inside of his home, plenty of places to play.

Walking forward, tongue busy and eyes closed to savour the other senses flooding my brain, I found the door with the heel of my foot and kicked backwards. The heavy wood slammed and locked into place.

James pulled his face back and hung off my shoulders to support himself. His hard cock pushed into my abs and his arse slipped forward in my hands, pressing, cheeks apart, against the bulge in my jeans. He smiled.

'Impressive,' he said.

I looked at him, casually, from eye to eye. Played it cool. Or at least tried to.

Truth is, I was already on fire and ready to explode. Blown away by his fancy house and burning over his choice of outfit. Or lack of.

In fact, it was taking more effort than I'd thought to silence the voices in my head. The ones telling me to rip apart his flimsy briefs and fuck him rough and raw against the purple and burgundy-striped papered walls.

But too much passion will give him the wrong idea. He needs to know where he stands. It's sex. Nothing more.

I kept my cool. Just.

'That's nothing,' I said, shifting him slightly in my arms to get a better hold. 'Wait until I've got you on your back and your feet behind my he–'

I couldn't finish my sentence. I didn't get a chance. His lips were against mine and we were kissing hard and deep again.

Evidently, I wasn't the only impatient one.

Opening one eye, I carried him towards a sweeping staircase that flowed down into the middle of the hall from a first-floor landing until I felt a soft, carpeted step under my trainer. Squeezing his arse I stuck my tongue as far into his mouth as I could. Then I lowered him onto his feet and pushed.

He fell. Painlessly on his side and looking up at me from the slant. His wild but innocent eyes still set on mine, like an obedient puppy waiting for his master's command.

His bare legs, covered in a soft ginger fluff, crossed each other, showing off the flawless curve of his perfect arse. His green t-shirt had fallen upwards and his fatless, pale six-pack looked as smooth as silk next to the cotton of his clothes and plush fibres of the floor.

Unfastening my jean button, I told him to pull down my zip. Without hesitating he pushed himself up to sitting and reached out towards my crotch. I slapped his hand away and he flinched.

'With your teeth,' I said.

His devilish grin returned in an instant and he placed his hands on my legs. Simultaneously he turned his lower body on his perch to face me. I tensed my quads under his grips and he squeezed tight in response.

Strong for a little guy.

Leaning forward slowly and opening his mouth at the same drawn-out speed, he moved toward the tiny, metallic rectangle. It was jutting out further than its maker had designed, what with the pressure behind. The top of his head obscured my line of sight but I knew he found it.

In the silent hall, I heard the almost inaudible click of his teeth against metal. Followed by the gentle buzz of an opening zipper. Then two flaps of denim bloomed open in front of his face and my jeans fell to my knees: my white briefs full.

He looked up at me. Eyes wide. Mouth hanging open a fraction. Waiting.

'Good boy,' I said. 'Now stay.'

For ten seconds, we said nothing. Did nothing. I was establishing dominance. Showing him who was in charge. That and I needed to calm myself before the storm. My balls already wanted to unload all over his sweet face.

I tried to ignore his adorable smirk and unwavering stare and the way he'd tilted his head to breathe in my crotch. It was harder than I'd thought. I busied myself by counting the freckles across the bridge of his nose. There were ten.

One for each second.

104

'Very good,' I said.

Then I pulled my briefs down to my knees. My cock sprung up and down and centred itself between us. He lowered his gaze. When he looked back up his eyes were wider than before. Filled with disbelief.

'It's huge,' he said.

Thinking back to some of our early text messages I laughed. A single, low, breathy laugh. A sound that said, 'I told you so'.

'Thanks,' I said.

Reaching out tentatively he froze a few centimetres from contact and looked up. I nodded. Then he wrapped his fingers around the middle of my shaft. Had to retighten his grip to make his fingers and thumb meet.

A pulse of pleasure shot down my legs and threatened my balance. Stifling the gasp attempting to escape my mouth, I centred myself by running a firm hand through his hair.

Sliding his grip towards me he peeled back my foreskin. I glided, wet and sticky with pre-cum. Then my millions of firing nerve endings blazed hot as he licked me clean.

Once. Twice. Three times.

First directly under the head, the tip of his tongue darting delicately around the ridge of skin attaching my foreskin to the rest of my cock. Then he flattened his tongue and licked me up one side. Then the other.

'Your pre-cum tastes amazing,' he said leaning back and wiping his mouth.

I shrugged away his compliment.

'Who told you to stop?'

'No one,' he said, smiling. He looked left to right. 'Do you want to go to my room?'

'Is anyone else in?'

'No.'

'Then not yet.'

'Ok.'

'Open your mouth.'

'I don't know if I can get that *in* my mouth.'

He was joking. Half-joking. But I didn't laugh. I repeated my command until he did as he was told.

'Stick out your tongue,' I said.

Again, he obliged.

Holding my cock at the base, I smacked myself against his soft, red muscle. Then I rested myself in his mouth with my hands on my waist.

'Suck,' I said.

For a split-second he didn't move. He closed his eyes and took a deep breath through his nose while my cock dribbled another bead of pre-cum over his eager taste buds.

I remembered how he'd told me via text, the evening after I'd flipped him around and pulled down his black school trousers in the deserted library toilets, that he'd never done anything with another lad. Told me how he lies awake at night, dreaming of the taste and the feel of a cock in his mouth.

He was savouring the moment. Sadly, the next few were worth forgetting.

James was a virgin. In every sense of the word. While his hole, tight as a vice, worked nicely in his favour, his cock sucking skills didn't. Take Adam, for example. All his practice in Mr. Price's passenger seat had paid off. This poor kid, on the other hand, was an amateur with a capital A.

106

His mouth was loose and lacked suction. His cheeks puffed out like a balloon. His gag reflex kicked in the moment he tried to go any deeper than my head. I watched him struggle and dribble until the inevitable scrape of teeth jolted me away.

'Sorry,' he said, his face turning pink with embarrassment. 'I don't know what I'm doing.'

Reaching down I held his chin gently between my thumb and index finger. Lifted it.

'Don't worry. Just do what I say.'

He nodded.

'Open your mouth and cover your teeth with your lips.' I laughed. 'Not that much. Just enough to cover your canines. That's better, good boy.'

Heat and wet enveloped me again as I slid myself carefully into his mouth.

'Close your lips around me ... Perfect ... Now suck. Gently ... Like a lollipop. Good. Use your tongue ... Do what you did before ... But don't lose suction ... Good. Keep doing that ... Make sure you breathe ... No, use your nose ... Good ... Very good.'

"Very" because James was a fast learner.

Before long he had his breath under control and his teeth safely tucked away. He was taking me further into his mouth without gagging; my cock hitting deeper and harder against the yielding flesh inside.

I wanted to watch every second. See every movement. Every detail. His thick red lips wrapped around me. The glistening tears filling in the corners of his eyes. His lean neck and shoulders and back below, blemish-free and toned.

But it was too much. I needed to distract myself or else I was going to unload fifty minutes early.

Letting my head hang back I opened my eyes, trying to ignore the body-shuddering build-up beating faster and faster through my shaft and around my balls. There was nothing but a chandelier and a white ceiling adorned with simple but stylish coving. Fancy, but not good enough. I could feel my load stirring. I wanted to look down so bad.

A large oil painting. It was hanging on the wall high to my right. Inside its expensive gold frame, a stern old man and woman in black. Grandparents most likely.

Perfect.

My cock stayed solid but my climax retreated as I thought about Grand-Mama and Grand-Papa looking down over their dutiful grandson, slurping away on his knees. Putting my hand on the back of his head I pulled him slowly towards me.

Inch by inch, the back of his throat squeezing tighter and tighter. A single tear falling down his pink cheek.

They'd be proud.

Then his fingers dug into my legs and his body convulsed. He pulled his head away, gagging and gasping for breath.

A thick, white strand of saliva connected my cock to his mouth before it broke in two. Half fell and stuck against his chin. The other plummeted toward the thick cream carpet below.

'Ok,' I said, looking down into his watering eyes and smiling face. 'Let's go to your bedroom.'

Twelve

Over the years I've spent a lot of time watching men.

Young, old, smooth, hairy. Large and small and average. African, Caucasian, Asian and Indian. Blond, brown, black, grey, red.

I've watched their arms and chests, legs and backs. Muscled, skinny, toned, broad, fat and slender. Their necks, shoulders, chins, mouths, noses, ears. Their eyes. Their hands. Their feet.

I've watched how they sit, how they stand, how they move. How they run and walk, jump and crouch, swim and sprint, stop and start. I've watched them play sport. Ride bikes. Drive cars. Read and write and work. Eat and drink and dance and fight. Shout and shove each other, full of testosterone.

Or hide away, shy and timid, where they think no-one's watching.

No two are the same, and, variety, as they say, is the spice of life. But, if you were to ask what my all-time favourite thing about a man is, one common feature that stands above the rest, I could answer in a heartbeat. Quicker than a heartbeat. I'd answer before you finished your sentence.

His arse.

Don't get me wrong, cocks come in at a very close second. No question. Especially long, thick, juicy ones dripping with pre-cum, or huge, mystery bulges aching to be unzipped. Cut or uncut, veined or not, I don't mind. But naked or fully clothed, a pair of pert cheeks gets me going faster than a bullet fired from a speeding train.

And James really did have the best I'd ever seen. At least back when I was eighteen. His was astonishing.

The kind of arse I could play with all night.

As he clambered to his feet and wiped away the strand of saliva from his chin that had moments before connected us, his empty lungs pulling in deep, refilling breaths, my balls tingled with anticipation.

I knew, the moment he ascended a few steps, his perfect little arse, coated in his spotless white briefs, would be level with my face. For however long it would take him to lead me up the grand, sweeping staircase, I would have the best view in town. Each delicious cheek mere inches from my mouth.

But I wasn't going to rush this part. I wanted to enjoy every brief second we had.

Kicking off my trainers, I pushed my jeans and underwear down to my ankles, stood out and to the side and bundled everything in my arms. Stuck my shoulders back and breathed in.

Looking my naked body up and down, his mouth hanging slightly open, he locked his eyes on mine. They shined even bluer through his tears. Tears that come after you've had your windpipe filled for the first time.

His panting subsided, he cleared his throat.

'You look great,' he said.

'Thanks.'

'Follow me.'

'Walk slow.'

He paused. Checked a grandfather clock ticking quietly to his right.

110

'We don't have long,' he said.

'I said walk slow.'

He paused again. Then grinned.

It took us three minutes to reach his room. Not because of the size of the house. Yes, it was big. Bigger than any I'd been in. It was exactly what you'd expect from an Edwardian manor house in the nice part of town.

The staircase reached up and to the right onto an open first floor that spanned the outline of the grand room below. Directly in front of the upper landing stretched a long, tall hallway illuminated by three miniature chandeliers hanging in a row.

Large, curtained windows, that in the daytime would no doubt reveal a finely manicured garden below, punctuated the right wall of the corridor. More old oil paintings in lavish frames dotted both. We passed a closed door of old, polished oak hiding an unknown room and reached a thinner, steeper spiral staircase, set into the wall and winding upwards. Leading to what James jokingly called his "wing".

Two fit boys could easily have made it up in under sixty seconds. Even at the pace we took. Slow and steady and unhurried. It's just by the time we were almost at the top of the second stairway, I couldn't help myself. On the narrow, twisting helix his arse was almost touching my face and the voices came back, unable to be silenced.

Throwing my bundle of clothes to the landing below I grabbed hold of his hips and stopped him in his tracks, four steps from the top. Then I moved my hands closer together until they cupped each cheek.

When he'd jumped into my arms his arse had felt great. But now, no longer compressed by his body weight, it felt even better. He had the supreme combination of muscle and fat. Toned but not hard. Soft but not flabby.

Reaching my fingers to his hip I grabbed hold and pushed his cheeks apart with my thumbs, playing with the warmth of his hole now less than a centimetre and two-millimetres of flimsy fabric away.

I squeezed him. Once. Twice. Three times.

The underwear has to go.

In a single movement, I pulled his briefs down to his feet, his hard cock thudding against his stomach. Then I took hold of his hips again and buried my face. Nose first. Slowly.

Closing my eyes, I felt his smooth skin against me. His arse cheeks were cool in comparison to the heat radiating against the tip of my nose. Taking a deep breath, I savoured his smell in the silky darkness.

Sweat. Soap. Boy hole.

My favourite.

Sticking out my tongue, I licked his entire crack, bottom to top. He shuddered and moaned into the air, high pitched, but not girly, as the sweet saltiness of his hole swept over my muscle and mingled with my saliva. I swallowed.

Then I ate.

Standing, I held his cheeks open and pushed and pushed my tongue against his hole as my lips kissed around it. He was jammed shut. Tight and pink and hairless. No matter how I poked and prodded I couldn't get inside even though his back was arched, pushing against me.

Too tense. But not for long.

Fifty aching seconds later, he finally gave in and I broke through.

The dull, hot, rust taste of blood-filled capillaries exploded over my tongue before flowing around my mouth and setting my brain on fire. I closed my lips around his wet hole and sucked. Then I pulled my head back, held his cheeks further apart and spat.

He had to hold onto the banister with one hand and push against the wall with the other to keep his balance as I enjoyed the view: my thick blob of bubbled spit dripping over his hole, down his crack and further down the inside of his skinny but toned left leg.

'Is everything ok?' he said, breathing heavily.

'Clean as a whistle.'

'Are you sure?'

I looked up. Over my hands and his arse cheeks. Up his back, still covered in his tight green t-shirt, to his craned neck and cute face. Into his wide eyes looking down at me, filled with a mixture of apprehension and excitement.

I smiled. Then I let go of his cheeks and spanked his right one, not hard, but hard enough to make a loud slap echo around the empty stairway.

'There's only one way to find out. Go.'

Past an adjoining bathroom his room was the size of a tennis court and looked like a cross between my living room and any teenager's bedroom.

On one side was a small L-shape sofa, a couple of beanbags, an old box TV probably passed down from Mummy and Daddy when they'd upgraded to whatever giant flat screen they now had in their personal cinema or entertainment quarter. On the other was a neat and tidy double bed with navy blue sheets, two navy blue pillows and a simple, wooden headboard against the wall. Wardrobes. Chest of drawers. Bedside table. A desk. A chair.

I hesitated. For a brief second, I was spoiled for choice. Then I remembered I didn't have time to waste and went for the easy option.

The bed.

Putting both hands around his waist I pushed him towards it. His short legs kept up with the acceleration and jumped in time with my lengthening arms. He landed on the mattress and bounced. Flat on his stomach, legs apart. His t-shirt had ridden up his back to reveal two muscled lines running up and under the rest of the fabric.

'Take it off,' I said.

Without a word, he pulled his shirt up and off and threw it to the floor. Then he wiggled higher up the bed and propped himself up on his elbows, still on his stomach. His bare back was curved in all the right places, and the bunches and bulges of his lean shoulders were blissfully accentuated by his porcelain, white skin.

'Very nice,' I said.

Reaching over to his bedside table he slid open the top drawer. Pulled out a small blue pump-tube of lube and a condom. Putting the foil in his mouth he tore it open and placed it on the back of his neck, directly under the sharp red line of his haircut. Then he placed the lube next to him on the bed and looked forward.

'I'm ready,' he said.

I was impressed: no doubt a move he'd picked up in porn. And right now, he looked like the industry's star actor. From his slim, blemish-free back, to his pert arse. His malleable legs and flexible frame. His long, thick cock pointing at me from under his balls. He was the total package.

Then he shifted his legs wider and I saw his hole. Red and tight and tiny.

114

I had no choice but to take my position over him, my knees pushing into the dark blue either side of his white thighs. My muscled legs, bigger than ever next to him, framed his arse in a V of smooth, young skin. The head of my cock rested against the dip of his cheeks.

Picking up the lube, I pumped it twice into my left hand. Then I threw the tube on the bed beside me and covered the translucent gel over my right index and middle fingers. Whatever remained I smeared between his legs and over his hole and around my cock.

'Chilly,' he said with a giggle, moving his arse from side to side.

I said nothing. I was thinking. We had forty minutes, max, before his parents returned with his brother, and I was in no rush to play happy upper-middle-class families. Take away ten for clean-up and getting dressed and five to fill him in about Adam left us with twenty-five. Twenty-five short minutes.

He took the first finger nicely.

Index. Smaller and thinner than the middle but still nice and thick. He winced and sucked in sharp breaths through his teeth as his slippery, soft inner tissue wrapped around me like a latex glove. But his hands stayed grasping at the bed sheets by his head. They didn't try to stop me.

I kept going, pushing until I felt the warm, gooey skin of his gooch against my knuckle and the hard but soft lump of his prostate against my fingertip. I curled my finger against it gently.

His hole clenched tighter and his body tensed as a wave of intensity rolled through him. I heard the squeak of fabric in his mouth and saw the miniscule hairs on his neck stand on end. He began to whimper, fast and loud through closed teeth, as I flicked at him from the inside.

'Breathe,' I said, as I pulled my finger out to the tip and slid it all the way back. 'Breathe.'

Like I said, he was a fast learner.

After a few minutes, his hold on the sheets relaxed and he lifted himself up slightly with his knees, his chest still flat on the bed. He began to rock his arse back and forth in time with my hand.

Reaching my free arm up I pulled his face towards me. His chest lifted and back arched, his arse pushing deeper onto my finger. The open condom fell to the bed next to him and I kissed him. Filled his mouth with my tongue. Then, still kissing, I pulled out my finger and pushed two back in.

His animal reactions kicked in and he tried to squirm away. I held him close, forcing him open from both ends. I knew he wanted it. His hungry mouth against mine was all the proof I needed.

He soon stopped wriggling, pushing through the pain until his breath warmed my face slower and slower and pleasure turned his whimpers into satisfied moans.

'That's it,' I said, resuming my position behind him and easing my fingers in and out. Slowly. Taking in every detail. 'Relax your hole. Concentrate on your breathing. Good boy.'

'It burns,' he said, half of his face pushing into the bed.

'It won't for much longer. Just relax,' I said.

Biting his lip, he closed his eyes and winced. Said, 'I'm trying.'

'Think about all the times you've laid awake in this bed. Fantasising about this.'

He closed his eyes and began to moan again.

'Think about all the times you've jerked off, dreaming about someone doing this to you,' I said.

'You. I've wanted you to do this to me.'

'So enjoy it. This isn't a dream.'

He nodded wildly and pushed his arse against my hand. I pushed as deep as I could in response and twisted my fingers gently. Crying in pain he writhed his arse away; my fingers flashing cold in the still air of his bedroom.

'Fuck that hurts,' he said, bundled into the foetal position; his white-knuckled hands gripping bedsheets.

I nodded and smiled at his flushed face, looking back at me through the right angle of his elbow propping up his hunched back.

'I know your pain. Trust me,' I said.

Eventually he smiled, nodded and resumed his position, flat on his stomach. Lowering myself onto his back, my abs rolling down pair by pair against lean, teen muscles, I kissed his neck. Just like I'd done all those weeks ago in the library toilets, fingering him against the cubicle wall. But in his parents' home our uniforms weren't in the way. My cock slid between his naked arse cheeks and rested a fraction of an inch from his hole. Turning his neck, he looked at me through one eye: his other cheek against the bed. Reached back and grabbed my cock. Then, holding me in his hand, he repeated the three words I'd wanted to hear again ever since we'd first met:

'Please. Fuck me.'

Thirteen

It's funny, really.

Funny how frustrated I became over how little time I had to fuck James. How stressed I was that the condom was too small. How impatient I became after a minute of fumbling slippery latex before running downstairs to grab my own I'd stupidly left in the back pocket of my jeans.

As I bit open the second packet, finally peeled the rubber down and lubed up, I could hear the seconds ticking away inside my head. With each stroke of my internal clock I knew I had less and less time to accomplish two very specific and important tasks.

The first, and least important, was to blow. Since watching Mr. Price run off into the sunset earlier that evening, the urge to unload had pulled and tugged at my balls like a greedy party boy after his first hit of poppers.

The problem was, as I put a hand on James' lower back to push his perfect, pink hole higher, positioned myself and checked the clock on top of his bedside table – four thin, red numbers blaring out the inescapable fact that his parents would be home in half an hour – I couldn't just rag him stupid, empty my balls and get out of there.

I couldn't do what Adam had done to me only days before. Use James like a personal cum dumpster until I was sweaty, spent and all better. It wasn't an option because of the second task. The most important.

He needs to enjoy it.

Not that I hadn't enjoyed having my arse ploughed by Adam, but I'd had plenty of practice taking cock. James hadn't. I needed him to push through the pain and want me again. I needed him to be keen to spread his legs for me so that one day, he'd let Adam join in.

James knew I packed a heavy punch, so to speak. But he didn't need weeks of picture messaging and a throatful to know Adam's would be heavier, bigger, thicker and stronger. Even the ginger midget knew the stories of girls not being able to talk or walk properly the day after one of the King's parties.

Everyone does.

There was nothing I could do but work James's hole hard and fast enough to get my rocks off, but gently and considerate enough so I wouldn't put the guy off bottoming forever.

Because let's face it, no matter how much he might have fantasised about my cock driving inside of him, balls deep, tough and rough, if I rushed or pushed too quickly or carelessly, the reality would incinerate his and my dreams in a searing, burning instant.

But, it was funny. Ironic, even. Because I'd severely overestimated how long I would last.

I should have known. Seen, or rather sensed it, when I'd slid my first finger inside of him. Past the constricted, ringed wall of his hole squeezing me so tight I'd felt the blood pumping under my nail, down my finger and through my hand.

I lasted four minutes. Maybe less. I didn't count. My mind was too busy switching control of my body to my balls, and they were too busy pulsing and throbbing. Filling up ready to fire as I pushed myself deeper and deeper inside the tightest boy I'd ever had the pleasure of breaking in.

I should have ignored his adorable whimpers and moans as his face turned redder and redder and droplets of sweat glistened across his forehead. I should have resisted the urge to push apart his arse cheeks with my index finger and thumb. I shouldn't have let myself see every single smooth detail of his hairless hole clamped around my rock-hard cock. Sliding back and forth, slow and steady. Pulling out and pushing in a little more each time.

About three-quarters the way in, time wise and physically in him, my load stirred. Fast and uncontrollable as waves of pleasure rose and rolled. Even paintings of his stern, wrinkled grandparents wouldn't have helped.

The veins in my cock bulged. My thrusts grew faster. Harder. Deeper. Rougher. Tougher.

Panic suddenly raced through my mind as I realised I could be hurting him. His hands were clutching at the bed sheets like little vices again. Bunching up the fabric in tall, skinny, creased mounds.

But my fear vanished as quickly as it had arrived. His eyes. They'd rolled to the back of his head, twisted ninety degrees flat against the bed, and only a thin white line showed beneath his full eyelashes. His moans were deep and slow. His body was relaxed enough to rock a counter-rhythm. His cock was hard. He was loving every second.

But so was I.

Putting a hand between his shoulder blades, I steadied myself and thrusted as deep as I could. His glutes, smooth and slick with sweat and lube squashed against the base of my abs and he took it all. Squeezed every inch of me from tip to base.

120

My other hand clamped around his waist and his back arched. His hole tightened. Mine tightened. My legs shook. My whole body did. His mouth opened wider to let out a loud moan. Mine joined alongside and our sounds filled his bedroom, bouncing against the walls and down and out into the house as my load did the same inside its latex bubble.

I don't know how long I laid on top of him afterwards, amazed at how quickly he'd made me cum. My cock twitching and his arse clenching. Our teenage smells mingling. Our chests rising and falling fast. Our hearts beating hard.

It wasn't ages, but it felt like forever.

When I eventually slid out of him the condom was full. James checked the clock and frowned. Told me to tie up the end and leave it on the side so he could jerk off with it when I was gone. I told him to send me a picture.

Five minutes later as I did up my laces, fully dressed and sitting on the edge of his bed, a toilet flushed. James walked back into his room, now pairing his green t-shirt with blue gym shorts. His face was still red but he was smiling from ear to ear.

Running over he jumped onto the bed bedside me. Threw his arms around my shoulders, hugged me and kissed me on the cheek.

'That was amazing,' he said. 'You're amazing.'

I smiled to myself. *Thank fuck he was a virgin.*

'Thanks,' I said, enjoying the warmth of his body against mine for a few seconds before casually wriggling away and standing up.

'Are you going?' he said.

'Soon. I should probably head before your folks get back,' I said.

'Yeah. I wish you didn't have to. We could cuddle.'

I suppressed a laugh. The poor lad really did have the wrong end of the stick. But it was too soon to crush his dreams. I rustled his hair instead.

'Another time. That thing I text you about though.'

'Oh yeah?' he said, jumping to his feet and following me out of his bedroom.

'You hear about Adam Stanmore today?' I said as we walked down the thin, spiral stairway.

His footsteps stopped behind me. I looked back. His mouth was wide in surprise.

'I know! I can't believe it!' he said following me again. 'Beaten up by his own father. What a prick.'

'Yeah,' I said, now back on the first floor and looking out the window, past my reflection, for signs of headlights.

None.

'You know why, right?' I said.

'Didn't he shag a girl in his parents' bed?'

I stopped at the top of the main, sweeping staircase and James almost bumped into me.

'What?' he said.

'No, he fucked a guy.'

'Fuck off!' he said, his face wide with surprise again. A lot wider than before. 'Who?'

I said nothing. Just looked down expressionless at him. It took him three seconds to put two and two together.

'You?' he said.

I nodded.

Then something happened. Another something I should have seen coming, but I'd been too preoccupied with getting my message across and getting out of his house to see it staring me in the face.

His mouth hung low and morphed into a frown. He looked down and then back up at me, trying to hide his emotions but failing. Like a child, he'd thought a few texts and a fuck meant we were boyfriends forever.

But this was different. This was extreme. The kid looked heartbroken.

'Why are you telling me this?' he said.

Shit. Think fast.

Putting an arm around his shoulder, I walked him down the sweeping staircase. Eyed a wall clock as we went. Now was not the time for damage control, but I had no choice.

'Look,' I said as we reached the ground floor. I squeezed him tighter and turned to face him, my hands on his shoulders. 'I wish I had more time to explain, but Adam meant nothing to me, I promise. But, we got chatting after school today. We spoke about what happened with his dad. I told him he wasn't alone and I'd be there to help if he needed it, you know?'

James nodded. Said nothing. His eyes still sad but now sparkling bright blue under the hanging chandelier. *Like Adam's had.*

'Then he asked me something really interesting. He wanted to know if there were any other guys at school like us,' I said.

James looked up. His sad eyes tinted with fear.

'Did you tell him about me?' he said.

'No way. But I said I did know one other guy. A really sweet, nice, cute guy I fancied the pants off, and before I knew it, the poor dude was begging me to get us all together.'

'Why?' he asked.

'I think he's lonely. Wouldn't you be?'

I opened the front door and leaned against it. James's frown had gone, replaced with confusion and sympathy.

'I guess so,' he said.

'So how about it?' I said, poking him gently in the centre of his chest. 'Shall I tell him he and I can come over some time when your parents are out? Hopefully for a little longer,' I said, tickling him.

He giggled and writhed away from me. Smiled.

'So you two aren't together?' he said.

'No way!' I said, putting my hands around his waist and pulling him close.

'And he won't say anything about me to anyone?'

'I assure you he won't.'

'Ok,' he said nodding. 'Why not!'

I beamed. Then I kissed him on the lips.

'You're amazing,' I said. 'Don't forget that pic.'

'I won't.'

Winking I turned and ran down the driveway, just as the gates began to rattle open. Almost diving behind a tree, I watched the black Mercedes pull back into the drive and trundle up to the house behind me.

Back by the bus stop I pulled out my phone. Thumbed a message to Adam:

I've got a bite. He'll need a little more convincing but his arse is tight as fuck. He thinks I'm his boyfriend. Will do anything for me. You'll like his house too.

Adam's reply didn't ping through my headphones until I was already off the bus.

You work quickly. Pics?

124

Scrolling through my archived conversations I found the picture message James had sent as I'd been walking home through the field after school. But as I went to forward it to Adam, a new one pinged across my screen. From James.

My load looked great as lube so I sent them both. This time Adam's reply was practically instantaneous.

Wow.

Fourteen

It's easy to see that at eighteen I wasn't living a virtuous
life.

Like most teenagers I had my motives and kept
them close to my chest. Trust and openness and honesty
weren't my strong suits, but unlike most, if I acted on my
vices, I didn't have a best friend or concerned parent to
help.

To bury me in guilt and shame or encouragement
and advice until I learned a valuable life lesson and became
a better person. I had no one.

And as far as I was concerned, virtues were for the
weak.

I got a rush from lying and manipulating. A thrill
from using others to get what I wanted. I believed it was
Darwin's Theory of Evolution at work. The strong survive
and the feeble perish. I craved the control and power my
actions gave me. The feeling like I mattered.

Like I existed.

It was a toxic way to live. I was lost and confused.
Cynical and uncaring. Angry at the world and everyone in
it. But at that puzzling, exciting and petrifying age, not yet
a man but one in law, it's easy to lose your way. Especially
if you're alone.

Patience, however, was a virtue I didn't outright
reject. It was one I battled with. Daily.

When I was a kid, when my folks were still together, every report card had said the same. "Oscar needs to slow down". "Needs to be more patient".

I'd never listen. Didn't for years. And it wasn't just at school. When my parents had split and I'd started to secretly explore my sexuality online, I'd always wanted more. A new guy. A new experience.

Now.

Then it had all changed. After I'd been caught in the bowling alley toilets and word had reached the corridors and classrooms. After they'd circled me in the school quad. After I'd limped fifty minutes to hospital and explained away my broken bones as a rugby injury.

It had been there, sat on the cold, sterile plastic hospital bed, seething with rage and hatred, before swallowing it down into the deepest, darkest recesses of my mind, was when I'd truly realised the importance of patience.

Soon.

That's what I told myself every morning and every night. Soon. Soon it would be over. Soon school would end and I could leave. Jump on a train. Find a job. Go to university. Somewhere sprawling and exciting and as far away from this dead-end town as possible. London. Edinburgh. Manchester.

Anywhere.

All I had to do was wait. Wait until I was old enough. Pass the time. Patiently.

Sat on the bus home from James's mansion, messaging two different boys, my balls empty and my cock asleep after a hard night's work, I had less than a year. Less than a year to ride out the misery.

Unsurprisingly, James and Adam were great distractions, even if the former was a concern. The next day, James texted endlessly. Asked how I was doing and what I was up to from the moment I'd woken up. Bombarded me with the kind of pointless drivel I'd done my best to avoid from kids like him.

My apprehensions soon vanished though. It turned out his parents were out more often than not: their social status dictating all sorts of dinners and fundraisers. After another superb night of ginger twink fucking, it seemed to me that if meaningless pleasantries meant an almost daily window to work on his tight, perfect hole, I had no objections.

Over the following two weeks, nine times out of ten, we had his place to ourselves. Every room. Every enormous space and expensive surface.

Once his brother was home, but it wasn't a problem. He stayed in the living room playing his Playstation. Gun shots and explosions ricocheting through the old, empty house. Completely oblivious.

Oblivious to the slurping and swallowing in the kitchen as his big brother practiced relaxing his gag reflex with my cock and fingers. Oblivious to my moans and groans as James took me deeper and deeper down his throat. Oblivious to the praise of his efforts dripping from my lips.

'Such a good boy.'

I was impressed with how quickly he applied himself. He wasn't just a fast learner, he was capable too. One finger became two. Two to three. Doggy to cowboy. Cowboy to reverse. Sideways. Standing. In the shower. Bent over the sofa, the bannister, his father's desk. Ankles behind my shoulders. Knees by his ears.

128

With each visit after school, James grew hungrier. He wanted my cock harder and faster, rougher and tougher, just as I'd hoped. And, to top it off, he warmed more and more to the idea of Adam.

He listened, with baited breath, as I bullshitted. Told him how happy Adam was that James trusted him. How much he looked forward to all three of us getting to know each other once his wounds had healed and his ribs were reset.

How "cute" Adam thought he was.

Naturally I didn't disclose what Adam really said to me. What he would tell me to do to James when I'd told him I was visiting. Which pictures to send.

Truth be told, Adam's secret commentary was a lifesaver. Especially when James wanted to talk or watch a movie and cuddle and I'd have no choice but to agree.

There were the other lads too. To distract me. Dan and Phil. The ones I'd messaged alongside James. At first, they'd been intrigued by my texts. But, ultimately, I couldn't convince them to play.

Dan didn't trust Adam to keep secrets, which I understood. When Adam "was straight" he hadn't exactly stayed quiet about his conquests. And it had only taken one morning for everyone to find out he was bi.

Phil hated him. Apparently. They'd fallen out years ago. When I'd told him that it was Adam Stanmore who I was interested in starting a three-way with, he'd said he would rather "cut his own balls off and eat them than be in the same room as that useless cunt".

But they all, James, Adam, Dan and Phil, paled in comparison to my biggest distraction. The distraction I had never imagined possible but had nevertheless fantasised about since my voice had broken.

Mr. Price.

My plan to snare him wasn't original. In fact, it was one of the oldest tricks in the book. Farcical even. I ran. Around the old creek field after school every day and before my inevitable trip to James's.

I preferred swimming to stay in shape, but it was a small price to pay if it meant spending an evening sweating in his proximity. I would walk home, change into my gym gear and, ten minutes later, feel the wind on my face, smell autumn in the air and hear the bustle of a busy park all around.

Dog walkers. Parents. Kids. All types of people when all I wanted was one.

The first evening, the one after I'd first spotted him, had been a failure. No sign of his hairy legs or broad shoulders and shaved head anywhere. After seven laps, I'd given up. Only had enough energy to let James ride me later that night. Let him unwittingly make up for the day's disappointments by blowing his load over my stomach and chest before peeling off my condom and sucking mine down.

The next day, Friday, had proved more fruitful. The sun had been up, swathing the crisp, cloudless evening with deep oranges, pinks and purples. We'd ran past each other and I'd ignored him. No eye contact.

I hadn't known if he'd looked but I'd felt something. Like heat over me.

Monday and Tuesday: nothing. Wednesday, I'd stopped to stretch a few feet from him. This time I'd looked his way and he'd looked back.

I'd smiled and nodded. A meaningless, friendly nod you'd give any stranger you happened to be sharing an interest with. He'd nodded back: no smile.

130

Thursday: no sign. Friday: we ran past each other again. This time I'd smiled, nodded and raised my eyebrows. The kind of movement that means nothing more than a recognition of each other. He'd done the same. Eye contact. Nod of the head.

Slight smile.

I got him the following Thursday, just over two weeks after I'd first spotted him. Two weeks of fucking James to get my abs looking their best. Two weeks of preparing and rehearsing exactly what to do and what to say. How to do it and when.

I was more than ready.

The old creek field was like any average English park. Large, rectangular, flat and green. Bordered on one side by tall oak trees behind a dried-out stream. A dark grey, potholed concrete path spanned its perimeter. Black bins and red bins for dog waste had been dotted about by the council. A small children's play area tucked into one corner.

We were on the long stretch. Me running east, him running west. We'd passed each other three times already. Smiled on the first. Ignored each other the second and third. He was twenty feet from me. No one else was around.

Fifteen feet: my heart beat faster. Ten feet: I saw a suitable pothole. Five feet: I planted my foot, twisted my ankle and threw up my arms.

Down I go.

The issue with faking a fall, however, is you have to hit the ground hard to make it convincing. An airy-fairy trip and stumble won't cut it. You need to chuck yourself down like a sack of shit. Solid, heavy and painful, which is exactly what I did.

'Fuck!' I shouted as I landed with a thud.

Rolling onto my right side I clasped my hands around my kneecap.

The fast one-two of trainers against concrete slowed to a walk. Deep, heavy breathing filled the air around me. A large hand touched my shoulder from above and behind. My balls tingled.

'Are you ok?'

Shivers ran through all of me. His deep, masculine voice. His touch. For a second the throbbing in my knee subsided, the blood rushing up and under my shorts instead.

'I'm fine,' I said quickly, turning to face him and flashing my best attempt at an embarrassed grin.

It worked. He grinned back, looming over me more gorgeous than ever. Every inch of him illuminated like a movie in the setting sun. I tried to stand. Could have easily, my knee was fine. A little grazed and bloodied but otherwise not a problem.

Obviously I fell straight back onto my arse.

'No, you're not,' he said, squatting next to me; his thick, juicy quads filling every seem of his tiny, black rugby shorts.

'Please, I'm fine,' I said.

'Is it just your knee?' he said ignoring my last comment like I'd hoped he would.

'I'm not sure. I think I might have pulled a muscle.'

'Where?'

Running my hand up my leg I wrapped my fingers around the inside of my groin. Squeezed. Winced. Opened my mouth a little. Moaned.

For a moment, he froze. Stared at my hand an inch from my package, bulging behind my flimsy running shorts. Then he looked into my eyes. At my mouth. I could smell him. Strong and salty but fresh.

132

'Here,' I said.

'Ouch,' he said. 'Can you stand?'

'Not easily.'

Standing he offered me his hand. Taking it I heaved myself to vertical, throwing in the appropriate theatrics as I went. Hobbling, I let him lead me to a green metal bench speckled with patches of dark, orange rust. I sat. He squatted in front of me. His face level with my sternum. My legs open wide in front of him.

'I used to teach sport,' he said. 'Do you want me to have a prod around? See if there's any damage?'

'No, it's fine.' *Hook.* 'Don't worry about it'. *Line.* 'I'll be ok.'

'Honestly, it's not a problem.'
Sinker.

'Well, if you don't mind,' I said casually, trying my hardest not to smile.

His hand was hot against my thigh. Hot and strong but gentle. He squeezed tentatively. Used the tips of his fingers to gently poke and massage muscle and tendon.

'You're fine here,' he said.

'A little higher,' I said.

'Here?'

'Higher.'

'Here?' he said, his thumb grazing my balls.

Gently biting my bottom lip, I winced. Arched my back a little. Clenched my arse. Opened my legs wider.

'Yeah, there,' I said between short, sharp gasps.

Locking his eyes on mine he began to knead. Slow and soft at first. Then harder. By now the park was almost empty. Only the occasional trill of bird song broke the steady in-and-out of our breath.

Everything was going to plan. Even better than planned. I hadn't even had to ask. He went ahead and came to my rescue like a knight in shining armour.

Thirty amazing seconds later, he stopped.

'How's that?' he said, placing his hands on his thighs and standing; his crotch now level with my mouth. 'Give it a go.'

'I can't,' I said, a smile stretching across my face.

'Don't worry, you won't hurt yourself. It probably feels worse than it is.'

'No,' I said, nodding down to my groin, my shorts full and my cock bulging across my other leg.

He looked down and his mouth hung a fraction.

'See?' I said.

Fifteen

The next five seconds were intense.

The sun had set. The air was still and silent. A late evening chill had forced the rest of the park-goers home and condensed our breath into slow, steady, steaming plumes. My heart thumped. My palms were sweaty.

In the purple of twilight, Tim Price and I were finally alone.

Touching distance.

Half of me loved it. Every nanosecond. Every shard of time chipping away. Every moment looking up at him. Over his swelling shorts, past his flat, strong abdomen; his wide, curved pecs; his powerful shoulders. Up past his rugged jaw and his thick, kissable lips to his eyes. His deep brown eyes.

My cock, full and thick and hard, stretched across my leg, pushing out the thin fabric coating my thigh. My mouth curled to one side in an embarrassed grin. My hands gripping the cold metal of the rusting, green bench to show off my biceps and triceps.

Miniscule compared to his.

But even though the man of my dreams was mere inches from my hands and mouth and body, the other half of me couldn't stand it. For those five agonising seconds, I was no longer in control. I wasn't calling the shots.

I'd successfully dangled the bait, but I couldn't force him to bite. I'd taken the horse to water, but was he thirsty? Up until that point it had been all me and now it wasn't. Regardless of what I said or did next, Mr. Price was in charge.

He had a decision to make. Would he stay? Or would he go?

Would he linger with the blushing boy in front of him? Abandon himself to primal urges. Let his body do the things he was dying every day to do. He didn't remember me. Why would he leave?

But he could.

He could have muttered some apologetic remark, turned on his heels and kept running. Hightail away before memories of his humiliated, broken wife tainted his reality and destroyed his desires. It was possible.

Probable.

No matter how much of a ravenous cock-sucker Adam had made him out to be, a voice in my head wouldn't let it go. Wouldn't stop reminding me that this guy had gone crazy.

I wasn't surprised that he hadn't remembered me. Sport wasn't exactly my forte. But back when he was just another sir, I remembered him. Every detail.

Mr. Price had never raised his voice. Never gotten angry. Never shouted or screamed without seriously good reason. Pricey had been the kind of teacher that had effortlessly commanded respect. The kind of sir that treated you like an equal. Spoke to you like an adult.

The one time he'd called me to his office was no different. Waiting to be told off for skipping class and longing to be sat on his lap. He was the kind of guy who only needed to widen his eyes and tilt his head to emphasise how unhappy he was. But he listened. Asked why. Gave a shit.

136

Then one morning, it had all changed. He'd been walking from the staff room, through the main quad, to the hall. Naturally I'd been watching his every step.

A group of year sevens had run past. Little, excited kids. One of them had caught Tim's arm with their rucksack and knocked his coffee out of his hands.

As porcelain had shattered against concrete so had he. All of his pain and fear and guilt, all of his secret shame bubbling away as his marriage was falling apart and his career dangled on a shoestring, had erupted in an explosion of sadness and loss and anger.

I'd watched it all. Gobsmacked. Even for him it hadn't been pretty. I'd even felt sorry for the kid.

A few days later, news had circulated that the kid's parents had pushed for the harshest punishment. After he'd cleared out his things, Mr. Price was gone.

The widely accepted theory had been stress. An early mid-life crisis, naively believed by children who didn't know any better. I'd been one of them. But while now I knew the real reason he'd broken down, I didn't know if he was roadworthy.

There was always a chance he would eventually recognise me. That I would stop being a jogger from the park and start being a very real reminder of his past.

No matter what kind of response I'd rehearsed and had ready in my head for what happened next, I knew I was playing with fire. I knew any moment all my planning and scheming could go up in flames and the last two weeks could be for nothing.

Fortunately, it seemed I had greatly overestimated how traumatic his experience had been. Mr. Price, I quickly learned, had adapted to his new life with the kind of vigour and energy you'd expect from a sports teacher.

'Well, well,' he said looking left to right.

We were alone. He squatted in front of me again. Reaching out he wrapped his fingers around the long, thick bulge in my shorts. I flinched with pleasure. He squeezed harder and I gasped quietly.

'You're a big boy, aren't you?' he said.

Practically beaming from ear to ear, I locked my eyes on his. Opened my legs wider. Tensed my quads and glutes and pushed my crotch into his hand.

Sweet success.

His grip tightened and I grinded myself against him. A wave of pleasure pulsed through me as a brief gust of wind raced by. Warm, wet pre-cum seeped onto my leg. A quiet moan dripped from my lips.

I relaxed back onto the bench and he released his grip. Stood up: his own shorts bulging so obviously in front of my face I almost dribbled.

'Is there anywhere we can go?' I said.

'And do what?'

Staring at his humungous bulge I said, 'Whatever you want.'

He looked left to right again. A new dog walker had appeared on the edge of the park and a large German Shephard was bolting across the grass away from us. It barked loudly, echoing through the empty park like gunfire. I watched his gaze follow it. Then he looked over my head. To the forest.

'Can you walk yet?'

Standing slowly, I stood. He was only three inches taller than me, but his broad, muscular body made him seem like a giant up close. Moving from foot to foot I fake winced a little. But not too much. I needed him to know I was malleable.

138

'Just about.'

'Follow me,' he said.

Within a minute we had crossed the field, traversed the dried-out creek and were quietly creeping into dense, dark forest. Trees tall and ancient and short and young surrounded us. Oaks or ashes or elms, I wasn't sure in the dim of the growing night.

They didn't matter. What mattered was that, from the outside world, we were invisible.

Twigs snapped and cracked as I followed his darkening silhouette; leaves and branches bristling and whipping against my bare legs. Soft, spongey, leaf-covered soil cushioned our tread and filled our nostrils with sweet scents of unspoilt earth mingling with hot, salty, evaporating sweat.

He stopped and half turned in my direction. Reached out his hand and I took it. Pulling me closer he led me around him. Turned me so I faced him. Pushed me gently against a wide, mossy tree trunk. Its soft coating squishing against my back like a thin, cold mattress.

My eyes had adjusted to the dark, but colour was gone. A mix of defined greys and blacks, he let go of my hand. Stood tall. Then he pulled the carpet from under me.

'I know who you are,' he said.

Keeping a straight face as best I could, and never more thankful for the veil of night, I shrugged my shoulders.

'Do you?' I said casually.

Calmly. My palms suddenly sweatier than ever. My heart beating in my throat.

'Yes, Oscar. You didn't think I'd recognise one of my students?'

I opened my mouth to speak. To continue my ruse. Make up some fake name. Lie through my teeth.

Apart from our encounter in his office, him and I had never spoken. How could he really remember me out of all those boys? He must have taught hundreds.

But then I remembered where I was. Where he'd led me. He'd known all along and here we were.

Throwing my hands up I pushed myself gently off the tree. Ran my fingertips down his chest. The hairs on my neck stood on end. His muscles felt amazing.

'You got me,' I said, standing so close our breath warmed each other's face. 'But I'm not one of your students anymore.'

He laughed, deep but quiet. Pushed me back against the tree with one hand. Then he leaned forward and propped himself up with an outstretched arm.

'Still an observant little so-and-so aren't you?' he said.

The sky above us black. The whites of his eyes slate grey.

I shrugged. Said, 'I thought you said I was a big boy.'

'You are,' he said, reaching out with his other hand and holding onto me again.

Keeping his eyes fixed on mine, his arm moved slowly back and forth.

'A very big boy,' he said.

'How come you played along?' I said, resisting the urge to pull down my shorts and briefs so I could feel skin on skin.

Heat on heat.

'It was cute. Pretending to hurt yourself so I would stop and talk to you. I thought I'd let you have some fun.'

140

'Bullshit,' I said, mostly sure he was bluffing.

He laughed again, his arm keeping its phenomenal rhythm.

Then he said, 'Ok. At first, I didn't recognise you. You were just a cute boy in need. But when you sat on the bench I had a flashback.'

I moaned quietly, electrified by his revelation.

'In your office,' I said.

He nodded. Said, 'Your eyes. They were so hungry.'

'They still are.'

'Is that so?'

I laughed. Said, 'I couldn't be more certain.'

'Good,' he said.

Letting go of me, he pushed himself back to vertical. Cocked his head like he was looking me up and down. I made out what I thought was a grin.

'How old are you now?' he said.

'Nineteen,' I lied.

'Good,' he said again.

Then he bent down and took off his left trainer. Began to unthread the lace.

'What are you doing?' I said.

He didn't answer. Just kept unthreading. Quickly but proficiently. Fabric twine whirred and scraped through the holes with each sharp pull.

Finished, he slipped the loose shoe back onto his foot, grabbed me by the arm and turned me around. Pulling my hands behind my back he tied my wrists together.

Tight. But not the tightest I'd ever had. I could wriggle out if I'd really wanted to. Then he flipped me back to face him.

This time he was smiling. I could see his teeth.

'I'm going to finally give you the punishment you deserved for skipping my class,' he said.

'Fuck yes,' I said.

Raising a single finger to his lips he shushed me. Then he placed his hand on his crotch, over his shorts, and gripped himself.

'Not a word. Understand?' he said.

I nodded. Fast. For the first time in my life I was more than happy to play any game he wanted.

'On your knees,' he said.

I did as I was told. The soil was cold but dry, giving under my bare knees. Twigs snapped. Grit and dirt stung at my bloody graze.

Placing a hand on the top of my head he ran this palm through my hair. Grabbed a tuft. Let go.

'You're going to take my load.'

I said nothing. Bit my tongue to stop myself asking how that could be a punishment. Checked that my hands were still restrained. They were.

'But you don't get a choice of where,' he said. 'You're going to open your throat for me and take every inch until I empty my balls into your stomach. Do I make myself clear?'

As each word vibrated through my ears my mouth hung more and more. My mind began racing at the thought of him using me like his personal property. His load hitting the back of my throat and filling me from the inside.

I must have nodded. I don't remember. I was living a dream.

'Good. Open wider.'

Sixteen

He started like he meant to go on.

Grabbing the front of my hair he pushed my head back. Firm but slow. In control. Dominating, but respectful. And only an inch, so my open mouth was at a better angle and I was looking where his eyes should be.

It was hard to see them in the greys of the forest and the silhouette of inky black above. I could make out his shape. His legs and his torso. His shoulders. Darker where his clothes were, a few hues lighter where his skin was. I could see his features. His mouth, his nose, his ears. I could hear his breath. Smell his scent.

But it was too dark to see his eyes.

Then they gleamed. Twinkled like far off stars. Reflected by a sudden burst of moonlight that must have escaped from the long, low autumn clouds I'd seen creeping into the sky before the sun had gone down. The silver filtered through thousands of outstretched branches in faint rays, strong enough to illuminate us in the darkness.

He smiled. So did I.

'Shut your eyes,' he said.

'Why?'

'Do as I say.'

I did as I was told. My lids descended and my other senses took over.

Thick fabric ruffled in front of me. Rugby shorts. They skimmed down hairy legs and a waft of warm air tickled my face. His scent grew instantly stronger. Then I flinched the tiniest of flinches as his hard, warm cock brushed against my chin, leaving a sticky bead of pre-cum.

I giggled. He smirked. Husky and through his nose. Then he pulled my head towards him. Into his crotch.

Hot and moist from his run he smelt phenomenal. Fresh and clean but strong. The kind of strength you can only find between a man's legs.

Taking a deep breath, I savoured him. Filled my lungs with every delicious moment since he'd last showered. Every layer of his day.

He let go and I rocked back to vertical. A twig cracked, echoing like a whip in the silent darkness, followed by the rustle of trainers on dead leaves. He was repositioning himself.

I licked my lips. Felt a hand on the back of my neck: my cue to open as wide as possible. Then he slid himself inside. As far as he could go. First time.

No messing around.

Adam had been a manageable challenge. And after giving James pointers, I really had no excuse. But as much as I tried, relaxed my throat and pushed my body towards him, angled my head left to right, anything I could think of, I couldn't get him down.

My mouth was watering plenty, practically gushing at the prospect of finally feeling and tasting Mr. Price, but even with the aid of his pre-cum my enthusiastic saliva glands still hadn't produced enough. Not to cover all of him.

His cock was huge. Like Adam's but thicker. Fuller. So full he hurt. He jammed into the top of my throat and refused to bend south, friction burning over me like I'd swallowed razor blades.

144

But then the discomfort vanished.

He pulled out, gathered a fresh layer of lubrication on the way and drove back inside. The walls of my throat squeezed and strained in retaliation. My fists clenched. My abs contracted. I willed my body to stay in control and not to convulse him out of me.

Victory.

Straight to the base. Shifting my voice box forward, all nine inches of him slid down until his sweaty pubes prickled my nostrils and my cock almost split the seams of my running shorts.

He filled me full. Like a glove. Like it was meant to be.

Grunting he quickly clasped both hands around my head, locking me in place. Strong and large and like dinner plates his hands covered my ears and muffled sound.

Every surge of blood became ten times louder: my heart beating through me like a drum. He began to rock my head back and forth onto him. Once, twice, three times, four. The slushing and sloshing deliciously amplified inside my skull. The rush of subservience surging over me as I surrendered, arms tied behind my back, to his power and his will.

Opening my eyes for the first time in minutes I watched the scene around me. It blurred up and down and up and down. Then it stopped.

'Fuck,' he said letting go of my head and pulling out.

Sound came rushing back, clear and crisp in the stillness, accompanied by the heave of my lungs sucking down air.

I wanted to ask if he was ok, though I was certain I'd kept my teeth safely tucked under my tongue and lips.

But I was too busy breathing. I'd held my breath for longer before. But not much.

'You alright?' I finally said.

'Yeah,' he said. 'I was close.'

'That's ok. I'm ready when you are.'

'No. I'm not done with you yet.'

Suppressing a smile, I opened my mouth and closed my eyes. Happiness rolling through me.

I knew our sojourn into the trees wasn't going to be a three-hour session followed by a feed, but it was nice to know I was getting more than a two-minute blow and go. *He's enjoying himself.*

I stuck out my tongue. Flat. He regained his hold and slid in. Over my tongue and back down my throat. But this time he started a counter rhythm. As he pushed my head away, he moved his hips backwards so his cock rested on my bottom lip. Then he pulled me back, thrusting his way down and squashing my lips against his abs.

Slapping my throat with his heavy balls. Filling every inch of me and then some.

He kept at it. Fucked my mouth slow and steady but rough and ruthlessly, my balls aching and my cock surging each time he stretched me. Then he grunted. Quietly, but uncontrollably. Sped up.

Faster and faster. Rougher and more ruthless until I couldn't breathe between thrusts. My oxygen quickly depleting, I took him for as long as my body and mind would let me.

Twenty-five of some of the most mind-blowing seconds of my life later, I finally gave in.

My gag reflex kicked through me, arching and shaking my whole body. Wrenching my head away I coughed and spluttered and hacked up a thick tendril of whipped-up foam. Pre-cum dribbled out of me as the sounds of my retching sent scintillatingly sordid shivers down my spine.

But Mr. Price was stricter than I'd remembered. He was having none of it. Quickly regaining his hold, one hand on the crown of my head and the other under my jaw to hold me open, he pulled me hard towards him. Forced my mouth back onto his shaft just as I'd gulped down the quickest of breaths.

Closing my eyes, I relaxed in his grip. Let him do all the work. Tensing my core and my spine I loosened my shoulders and neck but kept my back straight. Enjoyed the motion and my gurgling and his flavour in the darkness.

He grunted again. Deep and hoarse and louder than before. Then again. And again.

Soon he was grunting with each thrust. Thrusts that slammed his heavy balls against my bulging Adam's apple almost twice a second.

Fingertips dug into my head and tension released through my jaw muscles. Pain crushed into my temples. All of it mingled with the waves of intense pleasure radiating through me and setting my synapses ablaze like fireworks on the fourth of July.

The veins of his cock swelled against my tongue. His legs shook. He was close.

Only, there was a problem.

Some people think there's plenty of things wrong with blowjobs. The texture of cum. The taste. The temperature. The sting when it lands in your eye and millions of swimmers try to burrow into your cornea.

But, if you know and enjoy what you're doing, the only real problem is breathing. And with your windpipe filled to bursting, naturally it's impossible. When said blockage is a fat cock that's gaining momentum to pump a hot load directly into your stomach, the last thing either party wants is a break in the build-up.

But I'd never been in this situation before. Usually the guy would pull out and blow on my face. Or into my mouth so he could see it pool on my tongue. And while the thought of Tim Price unloading directly inside of me was like every Christmas coming at once, a panic began to grow. Tight inside my lungs.

I'm running out of air.

Fear prickled over me as I willed my mouth to stay open and my body to stay abandoned to his desires. I had to let him finish. No question. I couldn't pull away.

He's too close.

I needed to be the best boy I could be. An A-grade student so sir would think about me from dawn until dusk. From the moment he woke, to the moment he fell asleep. In his dreams. Wanting me. Needing me again and again and again.

But I still can't breathe.

His vice-like grip squeezed tighter. His body tensed all over. My eyes rolled to the back of my head and my heart beat exploded through me. He thrust forward one last time and pulled me so close my whole face squashed against his rippling stomach. Then he let out a long and low moan that vibrated through his cock, all the way down into my toes.

The fear and panic disappeared. The heavy dread in my chest dissipated. As his load streamed hot and thick into my stomach, heating me like whisky on a winter's day, I didn't care if I could breathe or not. My mind flicked into overdrive.

Nothing else matters.

148

I felt like I could have held my breath for hours as I savoured every sense. Every taste and texture, temperature, scent and sound, my jaw wide but no longer aching. It was only until he slid out, six heavenly seconds later, did my need for air regain its desperate struggle.

Bending over I opened my lungs. Deep, cold, salty mouthfuls seared my throat, catching and sticking at the cum lining my windpipe. I coughed and choked as the spin of the forest began to slow. A hand landed on my shoulder and steadied me. My breath regained its usual rhythm. I wiped my mouth and nose against my shoulder.

Looking up, in the black and grey of the blitz of trees and shrubs, I saw his towering shadow looming over me. Small, fast plumes of silver breath, illuminated in the moonlight, billowed from where his nostrils should have been as he pulled up his shorts, bent down and untied me. Then he laced his shoe and held out his hand, helping me to my feet.

'Need a ride home?' he said.

I nodded. Unable to speak. My voice almost completely gone.

For five minutes, neither of us spoke. I followed him. Out of the forest and back into the park.

We crossed the empty field as a bright, full moon beamed over us through a fifty-mile break in the clouds. Up the path's gravel path and out. Around the corner. Under yellow streetlamps and past a pub. Over a zebra crossing and down a left-hand street called Overslade Lane.

Fifteen houses down, a black Audi suddenly chirped awake. Its inside light flicked on. Its doors unlocked.

'This your place?' I said with a cough, shifting the last of my throat coating and swallowing it down.

'This is me,' he said, his car keys hanging off his finger.

'Are you sure you want to take me home now?' I said walking in between him and the car and leaning against the driver's door.

'Won't your parents be worried?' he said, smirking sexily under the lamplight.

'No.'

'Really?' he said, cocking his head.

Just like in the forest.

I smiled. Nodded and said nothing. He looked left and right and pressed the lock button on his car keys. No one was around as the car chirped again; its inside light fading to darkness. Reaching down he grabbed my cock, still semi hard under my shorts.

'I suppose you'd better come in,' he said.

Seventeen

Like most average towns in England, where I grew up was split into three.

The good. The bad. And the mundane.

James, my ginger twink, lived in the good. West and high on a hill where redundant old halls and stables had been converted into huge, red-brick homes complete with winding driveways and security gates.

My father and I lived in the bad. A stretch of land to the east. On the outskirts. Bulldozed and flattened for mass-built housing. All with the same cheap, rust-coloured brick and white, plastic rimmed windows. Crammed together and forgotten about.

Everything else was the mundane.

Boxy, bog-standard buildings. Some new, most dated. Some old and full of character but uncared for and unloved: weeds and rubbish tarnishing any potential. A few parks. An old creek. A couple of schools. Churches. A graveyard. All circling a town centre overrun with coffee-shop chains and charity shops, mobile phone stores and soulless clothing brands.

Mr. Price lived in the mundane.

Every street and lane had been set out practically identically by some sad, grey oligarchy. The same grey tarmac. The same yellow glaring out of the same dull metal streetlamps. The same attempt at a hanging basket or hedgerow to distract from the overflowing bins.

Every house with its own patch of grass or gravel or driveway. All with a back garden, walled off and hidden from the world. Curtains closed. "Beware of dog" signs. The occasional cat scuttling across the road. Everything about Overslade Lane was as unremarkable as anticipated.

His house, a two-storey terrace, suited the picture perfectly.

As his keys chimed inside a glass bowl and a light clicked on, it was like any other terrace house. There was a hallway with a staircase in front. A living room to the left with a sofa, coffee table and TV. Past the stairs was a dining room. Through the dining room was a kitchen. Tiled. Clean.

The only real difference between his and the places I'd found myself in since men had begun inviting me into them, was his was noticeably bare. There was furniture. Pretty much every household necessity. But all brand new. No scuffs or scratches. Factory-fresh smell.

There were a few photos but no artwork. No knickknacks or meaningful treasures dotted about. Instead there were plenty of empty nail heads poking out of plaster, bordered by rectangular patches of brighter paint. Or indents in the carpet where something heavy had stood.

Any other visitor would be forgiven in thinking it was a recent purchase. A new home freshly moved into. A blank canvas. But I could see the real story staring me in the face.

The story of a house that had once belonged to a man and wife. Spacious and close to town. Ideal for little feet to run around. A perfect existence. Until one day the man had betrayed his wife.

Hurt her beyond repair.

Enraged and broken she'd cleared him out. Took everything that wasn't nailed down, never to return. The man had no choice but to start his life afresh. How he wanted. The way it was meant to be.

'You ok?' he said, passing me a glass of ice cold water.

Jumping out of my daydream I took a long gulp. Its chill soothed my sore throat. Placing it on the oak dining table I watched him take a seat opposite me.

'Excellent,' I croaked.

'That throat of yours took one hell of a beating.'

I nodded. Eyes and smile wide. Said, 'It was worth it.'

And it was. Every ruthless thrust.

I had never thought I'd wind up at his house on the first day. One day definitely but not immediately. My initial plan had been to fall over and ask for a lift home. Suck him off in his car at best (I knew how much he enjoyed that) or get his number at worst.

But that.

Against a tree with my hands tied behind my back. His load in my stomach and my arse on his dining room chair. That was a remarkable result.

Surreal.

For a second, I couldn't help but entertain the idea that I'd choked to death, and with some stroke of sheer luck, found myself in heaven.

'What are you smiling at?' he said.

'Nothing,' I said, suddenly aware of his deep brown eyes on mine, rich like chocolate in the harsh light from a bare bulb overhead. 'I was thinking about earlier.'

'What about it?'

'It was a nice surprise,' I said.

'You can say that again,' he said, relaxing into his chair and placing both hands on top of his shaved head.

His biceps and triceps bulged out from under his t-shirt still darkened by sweat under his armpits.

'That was one of the best runs I've ever had,' he said.

Smirking I took my trainers off. Used my heels to slip them onto the floor. Then I reached towards him under the table with my right foot. Found his leg. Ran my foot up until I felt the hot, softness of his package under the thick black cotton of his rugby shorts. Kept my foot there, leg straight, until the softness became hard.

'Me too,' I said.

Taking my foot in his hands he lifted it so my heel pushed down onto his cock. He was almost as thick as my heel. He dug his thumbs into the sole of my foot and began to massage, grinding me against himself as he went.

'How's your knee?' he said.

'Much better,' I said enjoying the release running all the way up my legs and into my lower back.

'And your throat?'

Leaning forward I scooped up my glass, my hamstrings aching as I stretched. Took another sip of water, relaxed back and said, 'Getting there.'

'Good lad. I'll go easier on you next time.'

'Don't you fucking dare.'

For five seconds we stared at each other, our slow breath and sweaty scents mingling in the air around us. Him smirking like he was reliving every second of the last hour in his head. Me forcing my lips from reaching up to my ears as his words ricocheted through my mind.

Next time.

Then we both tried to speak but our sounds collided in an unintelligible mix of noise. He nodded. Me first.

'No please, sir, after you,' I said.

'Cheeky,' he said, lifting my foot and letting it fall back to the floor.

He looked me up and down. The half he could see above the table between us at least. Sat up in his chair, rearranged himself and cleared his throat.

'I was going to ask why your parents wouldn't be worried,' he said.

'What's it to you?' I said, channelling as much cheekiness as I could.

He smirked. Said, 'It's getting late.'

'Do you want me to leave?' I said, knowing full well he didn't.

'No,' he said, his eyes almost glazing over as two thick veins bulged up his arms.

Like he was grabbing onto something hard and long and thick under the table.

'You've only just got here. But I don't need some irate parent on my back,' he said.

'Don't worry about them.'

'As long as you're sure.'

'Positive,' I said.

'Good.'

Three letters formed in my throat and the word took shape. But before it flew out of my mouth I stopped myself. I didn't need to ask why. Why he was being paranoid about my parents.

I already knew the answer.

It seemed that while Mr. Price had taken to his new life as a confirmed bachelor with flying colours, picking up boys in the park and taking them back to his recently refurbished pad, he still had wounds. Scars from what had happened inside these walls.

I wondered where his bedroom was. If he and Adam had had any fun before venturing upstairs. In the living room. In the kitchen. On this table. I wondered if his wife had heard them. Or if she'd gone straight upstairs.

Wandered into her room like any other day. Found her husband on his back with a six-foot-six sixteen-year-old on top of him.

'Just moved in?' I said.

He narrowed his eyes on mine. Smiled. Laughed. A quick one-two from behind a closed mouth. Not forced but not gleeful. Like he'd been waiting for me to ask that specific question.

'You really are a sneaky little bugger, aren't you?' he said, still smiling.

I pulled my best confused face. Plastered it from chin to hairline. It helped that I was genuinely confused.

'What do you mean?' I said.

'Come on, Oscar. Give me some credit. I know you know.'

'I honestly don't know what you mean,' I said.

He frowned. Said, 'You really don't know?'

'Know what?'

He sighed long and deep. Rubbed the top of his head, his palm scratching against his stubble, and leaned back in his chair. Then he locked his eyes on me. Deadpan.

'My wife left me. She caught me in bed with another man. Took everything.'

'How was I supposed to know that?' I lied, relief flooding my body.

156

'I just assumed the news had trickled down. Everyone else knows. My family. Her family. My friends. People I used to call friends. Ex-colleagues.'

I suppressed another smile. Said, 'Is that why you left school?'

He nodded. Said, 'Pretty much.'

'If it makes you feel any better, no one at school knew. Or at least while I was there.'

'Was?'

'I'm nineteen, remember. I left last year.'

'To be honest I've given up caring what people think,' he said.

'Me too,' I said.

This time the words had come straight out. Two little pieces of truth inside my brilliant lie. Raising his eyebrows he leaned closer. Cocked his head to the side: his signature move.

'What do *you* mean?' he said.

'Nothing,' I said.

'Come on, sexy boy, tell me.'

Something strange happened next. My body tingled all over and the hairs on my arms stood on end. I'd had plenty of men call me sexy before. Handsome. Beautiful. Gorgeous. And I'd never tired of it.

But from him it was different. It felt different. I suddenly found myself talking. Unable to resist his deep, masculine, mystifying voice.

'I've given up caring what people think too,' I said.

'Already?'

'Age has nothing to do with it.'

'What people?' he said.

'My parents. The kids at school.'

'They knew–'

'That I'm a faggot?' I interrupted. 'Yup, they knew.'

'Don't say that word,' he said.

'Why not?'

'Just don't.'

We locked stares for another five seconds and I didn't have to guess what he was thinking. His eyes gave him away.

They burned with pain and sadness and fury. The same pain and sadness and fury I'd felt the first time I'd found myself on the receiving end of that hateful word.

For him it would have been worse. Everyone must have been so proud of rugby teacher Tim and his beautiful wife and their happy little life together.

Not anymore.

'They can all fuck themselves,' I said.

He nodded slowly. Said, 'How did they find out?'

'Long story,' I said, my stomach already knotting.

I tried to ignore the memories. Memories of that Monday morning. Their taunts echoing in my ears. The cold, wet grit of the quad soaking my shirt and scraping open my back. Their heavy black school shoes. The deafening cracks of my ribs.

Standing, he walked to the kitchen. A fridge door opened and glass rattled. One hiss. Another. Walking back in, he passed me a cold beer, its brown glass already misting over with condensation.

'We've got all night,' he said.

Eighteen

Fizzing and foaming across my tongue, the beer was cold and delicious.

It soothed my still burning throat as it poured into my stomach, mingling with whatever was left of the first gift Tim Price had given me that evening.

'It's a shit story,' I said.

'It can't be that shit,' he said, slumping back into his chair opposite me at the dining table.

'That's not what I meant,' I said before taking a bigger sip to try and loosen the knots twisting tighter. 'I mean it ain't pretty.'

'If you don't want to talk about it, we don't have to,' he said.

I nodded. Opened my mouth to speak. To change the subject.

Ask for a tour of his house. Get him on his feet and moving so I could brush up against him. Push my arse into his groin. Find somewhere comfy and horizontal where I could finally take off my running shorts and show him exactly how big a boy I was.

But the words didn't come.

Like he'd kicked a hornet's nest, memories began swarming angrily around my mind. The beat of their footsteps on concrete. The thunderous drone of their jeers booming through the red brick quad. The agonising stings of their kicks and stamps and smiles.

I couldn't look at him. Fixed my gaze on my beer bottle. Concentrated on its neck, moist with condensation, as the all too familiar rage began to simmer. I watched a stray water droplet lose its grip and hurtle south. Alone. Separated. Fragile. Saw it slow down over the bulge of the bottle before catching on the glossy paper label. I squashed it with my thumb.

'What's it to you anyway?' I said.

This time I looked up. Into his eyes still searing over me.

They softened as our gazes connected and a kindness glistened over their surfaces. It spread out across his face and into his strong jaw muscles, lifting them into a gentle smile. A smile unnoticeable from afar, say in the autumnal shadows of a park, but undeniable up close. Under the harsh bare bulb accentuating every one of his powerful features.

'Nothing,' he said before taking a sip of his beer. He placed his bottle gently and silently on the table. 'I told you about my wife, now it's your turn. I believe they call it a conversation.'

The corner of my lip curled into a grin. Now there was no denying Mr. Price was more than just a handsome face attached to a heavenly body. He was sexy *and* funny.

But it wasn't enough to change my tune. My mind was stuck on repeat, replaying scenes over and over in fast forward. Scenes I'd forced myself to forget and failed to yet again. Memories I'd pushed down to where all the other disappointments dwelled, safely buried alongside my parents.

Until now.

'I don't need your pity,' I said, placing my beer on the table harder than I'd intended.

160

Glass clapped loudly against wood in the night time still. His eyes darted down and back up.

'You won't get anything if you do that to my table again,' he said.

Then he smiled, playfully kicking me.

'Whoops,' I muttered.

'You haven't told anyone before have you?'

I shook my head. Words escaping me again.

I hadn't told anybody. Not a soul. Plenty of people knew. Plenty of people had watched it happen. Said nothing. Did nothing. But no one knew the whole story. No one had ever asked.

'It's good to talk,' he said.

'How would you know?'

He sighed. Quietly and quickly. Sipped his beer. Placed it back on the table harder this time.

'You think it was easy for me?' he said, his tone tougher but still open.

Firm but friendly. Once a teacher always a teacher.

'No,' I said, unable to stop myself sounding like a moody teenager caught smoking.

'And you know how I dealt with it? How I'm dealing with it?'

I shrugged and looked away. Toward the hallway and the front door. Anger bubbling hotter and heavier, sizzling over the sides.

I didn't run around a field every day for the last two weeks and given him the best blowjob of his life for a beer and a counselling session.

'I talked about it,' he continued, his gaze still burning over me.

I ignored him.

Patronising arsehole.

'I said I talked about it,' he said.

'Who with?' I said suddenly, twisting to face him. 'Your wife?'

'No. A therapist.'

For three seconds neither of us said anything. His face hard. Blank and uncaring. Just like when I'd first seen him in the park. When I'd smiled and winked and got nothing.

I gulped down a large swig of beer and the red haze began to lift, diluted by a rising panic. I'd forgotten where and who I was with, and why I'd ran around that stupid field in the first place.

'Sorry,' I said, tearing off a jagged strand of beer label.

Soaked through it peeled off the glass like a hot knife through butter, leaving a trail of gooey white paper bits.

'That was rude of me,' I said.

His smile returned. Bigger and more obvious. Said, 'It's ok. Let's talk about something else.'

'No,' I said. 'You're right. It's good to talk.'

'It is.'

'But I'll keep it short.'

'Short and sweet,' he said.

I nodded. Placed my almost empty bottle on the table. Wrapped both hands around it.

Gently squeezing the cold glass, I took a deep breath. Told myself to be like the bottle. To be hard and strong but see-through. He was obviously interested. In me. In my life. And that was a good sign.

The best.

But I had to be careful. I'd suppressed this for a reason: to be strong. I wasn't weak and beaten and broken anymore. The last thing I wanted was to talk too much. Undo my good work. Break down and shatter into a million razor sharp pieces.

'It happened about three months ago,' I said, relaxing my grip on the glass. 'I'd been chatting to this lad online.'

'Gaydar?' he said

'Yeah. You know it?'

He nodded. Smiled shyly. Said, 'I've heard of it. Haven't tried it.'

'Why not?'

'I don't know. I suppose I like meeting people in person. Call me old fashioned,' he said.

A wave of blood rushed south and filled my balls. Vivid flashbacks of the Old Creek forest gripped my body. My knee, still raw and muddy, pulsed in time with my heartbeat.

'Since when has tying up boys in public been old fashioned?'

'Oh forever,' he said with a wink before draining his beer. 'Want another?'

'Sure.'

'Keep talking. I can hear you from in there.'

'Ok,' I said, watching his perfect arse cheeks rise up and down under his tight, black rugby shorts and relieved to be free of his piercing gaze if only for a moment.

He walked into the kitchen.

'So, this guy,' I said, the fridge door suctioning open. 'He was my age.' Bottles clinked. 'We agreed to meet at the bowling alley out by the cinema.' Two hisses whispered into the room as metal caps were prised off. 'It was a Sunday so it was quiet. We played a couple of games. Had some fun in the toilets.'

Placing two fresh beers on the table he sat back down and slouched forward. A hot hand gripped my shin and lifted my leg to massage my other foot. His cock still solid.

'The bowling alley toilets. Good to know,' he said.

I nodded and took a swig of my new beer. It was a different brand. Sweeter but stronger.

'But we were caught,' I said.

'The staff?'

'No. They wouldn't care if you were dogging in the carpark.'

'Who?'

'This waste of space in the year below. Mark Jenkins. He walked into the toilets just as we came out of the cubicle.'

'Shit.'

'Yeah. Me with a boner running down my jean leg. The other kid all teary after trying to deep throat me and then gagging on my load. You don't have to be Sherlock Holmes to figure out what we'd been up to.'

'I remember that kid. Nerdy looking. Big thick black glasses?' he said.

'Yeah, that's him.'

'Harmless, surely? What did you say to him?'

'Nothing. We all froze. Then he legged it before I could say anything. I knew, then and there, shit was going to hit the fan.'

'Did it?'

'Big time,' I said. 'The next day he must have told anyone who would listen. All morning they whispered. Stared at me. Laughed. Pointed. Then at break a group of them came to find me.'

He nodded slowly. He knew what my school was like. How vicious boys can be when they're lumped together for years on end without any female interaction. How ugly things can turn when pack mentality kicks in.

'Where?' he said.

'The physics quad.'

'Did they hurt you?'

I wanted to say no. Shrug it off. Tell him I ran away. Make up some lie. I was done talking. Done remembering. Done feeling. Done forcing down the lump in my throat.

But my face was giving him all the answers he needed. He nodded, stopped massaging and softly placed his hand on the top of my foot.

'I'm sorry I wasn't there to help you,' he said.

'I told you I don't need your pity.'

'You're right,' he said. 'You don't. But I'm still sorry.'

I realised I'd been staring at my bottle again. I'd picked it up and was squeezing it so hard I was surprised it hadn't ripped open my hands. I looked up, into his eyes, and a warmth ran through me. Not hot, but warm. Warm and easy and simple.

Who knew it really is good to talk?

'They broke four of my ribs. Pushed me to the ground and stamped.'

He said nothing. His stare unwavering.

'I didn't even fight back. I just curled into a ball and waited for the teachers to break it up.'

'What happened?'

'The usual. The group all got detentions and a couple were suspended. I was told to get up and walk it off.

So I walked straight out of the school gates to the hospital. Told them it was a rugby accident.'

'Why?'

'It was easier.'

'It's nothing to be ashamed of.'

I laughed. Said, 'I'm not ashamed. I'm glad.'

'You're glad?'

'Yes. That Oscar doesn't exist anymore. The Oscar pretending to be straight and clinging to that lie. He was weak. And he died on that concrete. He's never coming back.'

For two seconds, he stared at me. Disbelief in his eyes. In that first second, I knew how he felt. I had no idea where that had come from either. But I felt better. Stronger and harder and more see-through.

I smiled. Shrugged.

'Anyway, that's my shit story and you were the first to hear it. Consider yourself lucky.'

He widened his eyes and took a large swig of beer. Said, 'I do. Very lucky. The worst I got was a few scratches when she caught me.'

'Ouch.'

'What did your parents say?' he said.

I shrugged again. Said, 'Nothing. Mum left when I was fourteen. Didn't say goodbye. Dad didn't even notice when I came home battered and bruised. He stopped caring about me a long time ago. But that's ok. He's a twat.'

'Wow,' he said, shaking his head.

'What?'

'You've had it tough, matey.'

'It's not all bad.'

'No?'

166

'No,' I said. 'No parents mean I can do whatever I want. Case in point.' I nodded. He nodded back. 'And, since I was so publicly outed, all the other boys struggling with their sexuality know who to add on MSN, don't they?'

He laughed. Loud and booming. Grabbed my foot with both hands and squeezed it hard. Dug his fingertips deep into my sole. My leg kicked out all by itself under the intensity, shaking the table. I wrenched my foot from his grip.

'Lucky fucker,' he said.

'I wouldn't say that.'

'Why not?'

Standing I picked up my beer and looked left to right. Locked my eyes on his.

'Well, for one, I've been here for almost an hour and you still haven't given me a tour.'

Nineteen

For a moment, he sat still.

Said nothing. Did nothing. Just kept staring at me through his sexy brown eyes as my suggestion of a tour trailed off into the silence of his dark and empty house.

It was in that moment, as memories of my past evaporated away, replaced by a ball-tingling present as powerful as his hairy legs open a metre away from my hands and mouth, I realised there could be an issue.

A big issue.

It had happened before, and like a complete idiot, I'd forgotten all about it.

Remember that silver daddy? The one who had taught me the invaluable lesson of sexual cleanliness? Who had delighted in driving me out of town to the city to get me to bury my face in the soft, spotless white pillows of a king-size bed so he could pull my arse cheeks apart and eat me out like he was dying of starvation?

That slice of heaven came to an end thanks to my chequered past. One minute I'd been riding his face, delighting in the scratch of his beard against my hole. Then, on a break, he'd asked me a few personal questions and the next thing he wanted to use his mouth for was talking.

Yapping on about my past. Asking all kinds of questions. Holding me close. Cuddling.

Gross.

But I couldn't stop thinking that maybe I'd done the same to Pricey. What if, after I'd shared my pathetic tale of woe, the insatiable hunger that had made him pump his nine-inch cock in and out of my eighteen-year-old throat was now replaced with an innate, paternal concern?

I'll be screwed and not in the good way.

The thing is, with some older guys, once the boy in front of them stops being a horny, care-free teenager willing to do whatever they tell them, and starts becoming a real person with real problems, there's nothing like the potential of exacerbating adolescent psychological trauma to make a hard cock flaccid.

I already knew a story like mine was the kind of story that did exactly that. Turned daddies into father figures. And it wasn't going to happen again. Under any circumstances. Especially with Mr. Price.

Fortunately for me, the ex-teacher still knew a thing or two about teenage boys. Namely that we're tougher than we look.

'You're right. How rude of me. It would be my pleasure,' he said, standing up and clinking his beer bottle against mine with a wink.

Walking next to me he placed his free hand on the small of my back and gestured with the other in no particular direction.

'After you,' he said.

'But it's your house,' I said, pushing my body an inch closer into his and twisting my neck so our nose and lips were almost touching.

He smelt extraordinary. Sweet and salty and musky all at the same time. So good my saliva glands kicked into overdrive and I had no choice but to swallow their fresh batch straight down before it dripped out the corner of my grinning mouth.

'Well done,' he said, skimming his hand down my back and onto my arse.

He cupped a feel of my right cheek. A full feel. So full his little finger slipped between my crack, warming my hole through the flimsy fabric of my running shorts.

'But how will I be able to watch this if I'm showing you the way?' he said.

'Excellent point, sir,' I said, arching my back a little.

Enough to let him know I was happy with the way we were heading.

'I like it when you call me sir,' he whispered into my ear.

'Good to know. Sir.'

Leading the way, I checked out the kitchen first. It was nothing special. Just your average English terrace layout, modernised with a matt-finish chrome worktop and a stainless-steel fridge-freezer. The only nonessential additions were a collection of multi-coloured cook books neatly stacked on a corner shelf next to a surprisingly full spice rack.

'I've been teaching myself to cook now that I'm fending for myself,' he said.

'She did it all?'

'All of it. She wanted to. I never lifted a finger in here,' he said, leaning on the worktop with both hands; his biceps and triceps bulging alongside the thick veins in his arms as his mind was momentarily lost in thought. 'It's funny though.'

'What?' I said.

'I fucking hated her cooking.'

We laughed in unison. Loud and boisterous, fuelled by the prickle of alcohol.

Our beers were almost empty so we drained them. He passed me his empty bottle to throw in the recycling while the fridge suctioned open for a third time and a brand new, icy cold bottle was passed my way.

'You any good then?' I said.

'At cooking?'

I nodded.

'Awful,' he said.

'Well,' I said, lifting my bottle. 'Here's to eating out.'

'To eating out,' he said with a mischievous wink as we toasted; glass on glass clinking and echoing gently against the gleaming white splashback tiles.

'The garden out there?' I said gesturing to a curtain-less window, that in the darkness of outside and the brightness of in, showed nothing but mirrored versions of ourselves and the kitchen around us.

'Yeah but it's a shit tip,' he said, maintaining his stare at our reflection. 'Another thing she looked after.'

Reaching out he pulled me into him. Back first so we could both see ourselves. My arse finally pushing into his groin.

I watched his huge arms wrap around me. One hand over my pecs and the other on my stomach, tracing my six-pack down. Down under my shorts but over my briefs.

My body shuddered against his as he squeezed my package. His fingers dancing over my shaft, expanding by the second under my white cotton briefs and running shorts. His lips kissed my neck. My cheek. His own package growing and pushing into me.

'This view is much better,' he said.

'Much,' I said, wriggling out of his hold and smirking: I wasn't done with the tour.

Next was the living room. Again, I led the way. Him no more than a foot from me. Close enough so we could still feel each other's heat and smell each other's scents. But far enough so he could cock his head to the side and burn his gaze all over me.

Flicking on the light I saw a blend of cream walls and slate grey carpet materialise. Like the dining room and kitchen, it was nothing special. Larger than both (separately, not combined) it had everything you'd expect to find in a living room.

TV. Bookcase: empty bar three indistinguishable hardbacks. An old fireplace, bricked-in and replaced with a modern gas burner. A coffee table.

The sofa, however, was the perfect place for a pit-stop. Great size and plush looking fabric. Three seats in a masculine light grey. Unmistakably new.

Perching on the armrest I faced him and hooked my legs around his thick calves. Reached out towards his towering body and grabbed a hold of his t-shirt. Bunched it inside my fist and pulled him into me.

We kissed. Hard and deep. Our tongues playing and our hands exploring. Only the soft slurps of our lips and the occasional, uncontrollable moan escaping my mouth filled the room around us.

A few minutes later he pulled back. Only a fraction.

'This tour's going to take all night at this rate,' he said.

'That's fine by me.'

He came at me again and we kept kissing. Raising my chin, I let him at my neck. Relaxed my spine and shoulders and sunk into his hold. One hand on my waist, the other on my neck. His kisses soft but ravenous. His grip tender but strong.

Pushing myself backwards off his thick pecs, hard and strong like warm maple, I landed on the plush cushions of the sofa with my legs dangling over the armrest. Following me around he stood, crotch level with my face and looked down.

'What are you smiling at?' he said, grabbing hold of the thick mound of pushed-up fabric running from his groin to pocket.

'Nothing, sir,' I said, trying my best to stop my eyes popping out of their sockets at the vision in front of me.

For the first time that night, in the light of another bare bulb blazing behind him, I could see just how impressive his bulge was. Rock hard and almost ripping open the seams of his shorts. Shorts designed to withstand the strength and strain of a team of rugby players grasping and gripping at them at full speed.

'Really?' he said, keeping his grip on himself and reaching out towards me with his other hand.

It landed on my crown. Ran through my thick brown hair and down my cheek. Across my chin. Over my mouth.

Then his thick fingers pushed open my lips, my teeth obeying simultaneously, and smeared the delicious saltiness of his skin down my tongue.

Wrapping my lips around them I sucked. Nodded.

By the time he was almost done playing with my mouth, his shorts and boxer briefs were down by his ankles and his knuckles were resting against my front teeth. My shirt was off and my own shorts and briefs were by my knees, locking my legs together over the armrest.

His eyes were on fire. Searing over every detail and movement. My tensed biceps as I slowly jerked myself. My convulsing abs each time he pushed his fingertips down my throat and flicked upwards to make me gag. My free hand slowly rubbing my overflowing saliva down my chest and over my six-pack.

His free hand full of himself, stroking up and down at the same speed as me.

Then he pulled his fingers out. Replaced them wordlessly with his cock. My eyes rolled into the back of my head and time ceased to exist.

'Good boy,' he said. 'Just like that.'

In the darkness, I listened to his commentary. Like I'd done at school, back when I had no choice but to attend PE classes. Back when I still wondered why every time I saw him I'd felt a weird feeling in my stomach.

But now, instead of blushing at the blood running south, I abandoned myself to the sound of his deep and commanding voice. I let it fill my ears as the tastes and textures of his throbbing cock filled my mouth.

'Fuck, Oscar … You are such a good boy. Such a good boy … That's right, keep stroking yourself … Slower. Yes. Good boy. In time with me … Yes … Open wider. That's it. Take it down. All of it. Hold your breath … Good boy. Gag for me. Good boy. Good boy.'

I had to stop my hand. The last time I'd blown was almost twenty-four hours ago and each time he'd told me how good I was my balls had contracted and my cock had almost burst. Each time he'd praised me my load had rumbled, ready to be free.

Way too soon.

'What's wrong?' he said, sliding out of my mouth.

'I'm going to blow if you keep calling me a good boy,' I said, licking up his glaze from my lips.

'In that case,' he said, pulling up his shorts, bending down and filling my mouth with his tongue to taste himself. 'I'd better take you upstairs and finish this tour.'

Twenty

We didn't make it upstairs. Not right away.

First there was the hallway. The same dark, narrow passage we'd walked through from the street just over half an hour ago. But this time we came from the living room. And this time a strong hand on the end of a stronger arm pushed me from behind, up against the wall.

I hit the smooth, cold surface hard, but managed to get my hands up to brace myself just in time. My body thudded painlessly against brick and plaster and wallpaper as my shorts and briefs were dragged down to my ankles, fabric whispering over hair and muscle.

A single word left his mouth, no less than a foot from my ear. The three syllables echoing in the quiet of the house, deep and masculine and hypnotising, floating on the sticky, salty heat of our bodies.

'Beautiful.'

I didn't need to look behind to know what he was looking at. What he was thinking. What he wanted. Now done with my throat Mr. Price's fingers needed a new hole to play with.

'All yours, sir,' I said, twisting my neck to look into his dazzling eyes; my back arching and pushing my naked arse towards him.

From that moment on, my arse was his. Every curve. Every inch of tight and soft-where-it-counts muscle. All of it. Because even though I'd maintained a strict

176

grooming standard to ensure nothing but a smooth welcome, it had been too long since I'd had a visitor.

My ginger wannabe-boyfriend James had been great fun. And still was. My balls still twitched every time I thought about the flawless white cheeks on his face turning red as I'd pulled the ones below apart and broken his cherry. But I'd turned him into a hungry bottom. He was far too busy dealing with what I had to give to dish it back out.

Adam had been my last top. Two-and-a-half weeks ago. After getting ruthlessly pounded on all fours by the captain of the rugby team on his parents' bed, at this point I was craving cock up my arse like an addict in rehab.

What was surprising, however, was what happened next. Not Mr. Price pinning me against the wall as his free hand traced the ridge of muscle down my back and over my bare arse cheeks. Or the sound of saliva gathering or the clap of it landing in his palm or the warm wetness of him smearing it over my hole. It's how he did it. How he fingered me.

He was good. Very good.

I'd had guys like Mr. Price before. Recently turned or in the process of. They were often the easiest to find online. Always eager to explore the new them. Their dirty, filthy, sinful dark side raring to have its way with me, the blue-eyed, teenage twink.

But a couple, understandably, had been a little hasty. A little too rough. Too impatient. Used to a self-lubricating hole and unaccustomed to the potential of searing pain an untrimmed nail or overenthusiastic finger away.

And yes, I was prepared to be biased. Somewhat forgiving of Mr. Price. Especially after I'd dreamed and fantasised and prayed this very scene would happen. And yes, after he'd spent the evening tying me up with his trainer lace before skull fucking me to within an inch of my life, you can't blame me for thinking the guy would be ravenous.

But as he wrapped his left arm under my armpit and around my pecs and held me into his body, his mouth and tongue lapping hungrily against my ear, his right hand was adept. Expertly capable with a blissful balance of both care and carnal desire.

His finger was slow. Steady. Well lubricated by a perfect combination of his spit and my sweat. It pushed inside of me like it belonged there. Curled and flicked like it knew the terrain as well as the back of the hand it was attached to.

Then one finger became two. Middle joined by index. I had no choice but to surrender to his strength and skill, arching my back as far as I could to let him reach deeper as my pre-cum dribbled down, staining the papered walls.

'You're so fucking good at this,' I said.

'Just you wait, boy,' he said pushing so hard a short, sharp gasp forced itself out of my mouth and my head lulled back onto his thick shoulders.

Lifting my arms, I hung off his bicep wrapped around my chest. Dug my fingertips into the hard, tensed muscles of his forearm. Relaxed my body against his wide, well-built pecs. Turned my neck and found his lips.

We kissed fast and deep. Our tongues dancing to the rhythm of his fingers.

Then he pulled out. Spanked my arse cheek as my hole shut tight. Squeezed me even closer and reached around my torso. Found my mouth and made me clean his fingers.

Delicious.

'Upstairs,' he said, ten seconds later.

We still didn't make it to the bedroom.

Next was the upstairs landing. Just your average, bog-standard rectangular-ish, first-storey landing. Carpeted with a thin layer of worn fibres. Probably once red or burgundy, now a dull brown, but clean and maintained. Three closed doors stood east, north and west at the top of the stairway. A bathroom and two bedrooms, I assumed.

Not that I got a chance to find out. My shorts and briefs in a crumpled heap at the bottom of the stairs next to my socks and trainers, I'd taken the steps slowly. Leading the way again. Lifting my shirt, my last piece of clothing, above my head as he'd followed.

My arse, almost level with his face. My back, muscled but slender. Young and flawless. It had been too much for him. He'd pushed me again. Right at the top. Bent me over the last few stairs, exactly like I'd done to James only days ago.

For a split-second, I wondered what James was doing. All alone in that big house in the good part of town. He would definitely have texted me by now. Staring at his phone. Wondering why I hadn't showed like I'd said I would.

Sadly for him, my phone was at home. My front door key safely nestled in the zip pocket of my shorts was the only thing I'd taken with me on my run.

Then I forgot all about James. As quickly as he'd popped into my head: an instant. Two huge hands landed on my arse. A cheek each. They pulled away from each other and held me open, forcing me back to reality.

Open just long enough for him to take in the view and for a waft of cool air to tickle my wet crack. Long enough for me to smile to myself. I'd seen what was coming a mile off.

He'd been desperate to eat me out downstairs. After he'd pulled his fingers out and spanked me.

Obviously with my face to the wall, I hadn't been able to see him, but I'd sensed him look down. I'd felt his body momentarily freeze behind me, struggling with a decision, before eventually giving it up.

A part of me had thought he'd pussied out. That maybe he hadn't explored far enough into his dark side yet to upgrade fingers to lips and mouth and tongue. Especially after I'd been running. I'd douched, thankfully, but I was fairly sweaty.

I was also wrong: the answer simple. Downstairs in the hall there hadn't been enough room.

At six-foot I'm not exactly the smallest of boys. And at six-foot-three and built like the rugby coach he was, it would have been a tight fit. He could have done it. Got on his knees and gone to town as I'd pushed off the wall and shoved my arse into his face.

But at that angle your neck gives out way before either of you have had your fill. And with half my body now flat on the carpet and the rest inclined down, the position couldn't have been beaten. He would be able to grind his tongue and lips and stubble in and around my salty boy hole as much as he wanted.

And he did.

For how long I don't know. I couldn't think of anything else other than the sounds of him sucking and slurping and the feeling of pure submission as he pulled at my arse and buried his face and nose as deep as he could.

180

The smell of clean but old carpet filling my nostrils. The dull, coppery taste of my hole still tingling on my tongue from his fingers. I was on Cloud Nine.

Now and again I looked back and my whole body would shudder and tense. Pleasure and excitement would take hold and the miniscule hairs on my neck and shoulders and back would stand on end at the sight of the hunger and awe in his eyes. His shaved head never looking better than between my cheeks. His huge arms like glorious wings either side of his powerful shoulders.

'I've got to take you to my bedroom,' he said pulling his head back before pushing himself in a press-up motion up to standing.

'What's wrong with right here, sir?' I said, twisting my body to find him reaching up a hand. 'You can fuck me wherever you want.'

'No. Not here. Come on,' he said.

Shrugging, I wrapped my fingers around his wrist and hauled myself up. Me completely naked. Him fully dressed, three steps below. Facing each other.

My cock, long and hard and straight, poking him in the sternum.

He smiled. Raised his eyebrows. Excitement flickered across the two hazel-ringed spheres below. But a different kind of excitement. Not the kind I'd just watched.

It was like I was looking at a big kid itching to show off a new toy.

'What?' I said.

'You'll like my bedroom.'

Turning I said nothing. Didn't have an answer. For the first time that night I had doubt instead. Not about fucking him. Not in a million years. Just what he'd said. I would "like his bedroom".

Yeah right.

Going by the state of the rest of his house there would need to be a leather sling and a live-in, donkey-dicked houseboy carrying a golden tray of weed to make up for the serious lack of style and comfort.

Three seconds and a click of a dimmer switch later, however, he made perfect sense.

'Wow,' I said as more light bathed the scene in front of me.

'Right?'

'But, the rest of the house.'

'Is a work in progress, I know.'

'I was going to say shit hole.'

He laughed. Said, 'Since she left I've been doing the place one room at a time. This one seemed like the obvious first choice. Too many bad memories. You like it?'

'It's fucking sexy.'

And it was sexy. It was dark and masculine and spacious and contemporary. Like walking into a magazine spread.

Polished oak floorboards. A ceiling, stripped back to reveal sturdy beams slicing the space above into ten narrow sections of white plaster and dark tan wood. Every item from the sturdy wardrobe to the full-length mirror, desk and leather armchair, spotless and expensive in the light from twisted bulbs inside stylish charcoal grey shades.

The bed, of course, was the main event. A huge king, covered in expensive white sheets and plush white pillows. Flanked either side by bedside tables on skinny, tapered legs supporting sophisticated lamps.

There was absolutely no doubt in my mind. I did like his bedroom.

I liked it for the obvious reasons. Soon I would be on those sheets. Rolling around like a pig in shit with the man of my dreams buried nine inches inside of me. But also because, in a fleeting, abstract way, I could relate to it. It didn't belong here. Not in this house and not in this part of town.

Not in this town at all.

'You alright?' he said, now shirtless.

Looking his ball-burstingly perfect torso up and down, I smiled. Thought about him being caught by his wife in this room. And how later, piecing his life back together, he'd gutted it. Recreated it in his stunning image. I nodded my head at the bed.

'Couldn't be better. Let's make some new memories.'

Twenty-one

T hen my life changed.

Mr. Price and I did, until only weeks ago, what I'd believed was only ever going to happen in my wildest of wet dreams.

What I'd wanted him to do to me since I'd first laid eyes on him. What I'd thought about for years. In the classroom. On the sports field. Lying awake at night, beating myself off or simply staring at the grey ceiling, concocting steamy fantasies in my head.

Farfetched little fictions to help me fall asleep.

Stories to convince myself life would get better. That maybe, just maybe, there was a chance something could grow out of the barren wastelands of putrid shit I called home. Something beautiful and exciting and different. Something to make me forget about the kids at school and the cold, dark void left by my parents.

Watching him peel his rugby shorts down his legs, I pinched myself. I had to make sure I wasn't dreaming. Because now those farfetched little fictions weren't so farfetched or fictional anymore.

I can't believe this is happening.

And the best part? Mr. Price was better than all my hopes and wishes combined.

He rocked my fucking world.

He started on top. Both of us naked. Him kneeling between my legs, picking up my calves and resting them on his shoulders. His smooth muscles almost gold under the dimmed light. Me on my back in the middle of the king-size bed. The expensive white, Egyptian cotton sheets soft against my skin. A plush pillow supporting my head and neck.

My young, toned body his.

Turning his head to the side, he kissed the inside of my thigh a fraction below my knee. His jaw strong and straight. Then he edged closer, until his torso pushed against the backs of my thighs; their position mimicking the perfectly defined V of his wide, hairy six-pack.

His cock on top of mine. His balls against my arse.

A curious thought struck me. Usually I would have crawled onto the bed. Hands and knees. Back arched. Looking behind with an irresistible smile, beckoning whoever it was forward. Then I'd bend my elbows and lower my upper body to make a wedge shape: the best position for maximum power and convenient access. My go-to. But I hadn't with him.

For two reasons.

The first was that when I said he was a big boy, I meant it. Adam's cock was longer but Tim's was thicker. Too much girth to take from any old angle. And legs up mean you can spread them wider. And wider spread legs mean a more flexible hole.

But, comfort aside, there was a more important reason. It didn't feel right. Mr. Price wasn't some random hook-up. He wasn't some guy I'd met online who'd told me to be waiting arse up and face down.

He was more than that. He was literally a dream come true and I wanted to watch every real second. See all the action.

'You've got to stop looking at me like that,' he said, shaking his head.

'Or what?'

'Or else I'll blow in about two seconds.'

'I'm sure you can handle it, sir,' I said, sticking out my tongue.

He shook his head again. Quickly. Made a noise. Grunted like a rugby player psyching himself up before a game.

'Open the drawer,' he said, nodding toward the bedside table.

His hands were busy. Stroking. One up and down his own rock-solid shaft. The other up and down mine, making my balls tingle and my pre-cum dribble up and out and onto the side of his index finger curled around me.

Reaching over I felt my way until the metal knob of the bedside table chilled my fingertips. Pulling open the drawer I lowered my hand inside like one of those toy crane machines you get at fairs or service stations. Found what he wanted.

Condoms and lube. Crinkle-cut-edged plastic squares and a small plastic tube. Picking them up slowly I brought my hand up and back around and placed the contents on my chest. Never once breaking eye contact.

I reached out again and the drawer closed shut with a gentle clap of wood on wood.

Bending forward he kissed me, testing my flexibility at the same time. He pushed my legs down with his body until the fronts of my thighs met my abs and pecs and my knees were in line with my shoulders; the plastic pump tube of lubricant digging into our chests.

His tongue buried itself inside my mouth and his elbows came to rest either side of my head. Our cocks grinding. Our breath and scents mingling. Sweat and beer and boys.

Slowly pushing himself back, he picked up a condom from between my pecs. Placed the top edge between his teeth and ripped it open in one, slick movement. Then he discarded the wrapper and peeled the thin, glossy latex around himself. I didn't recognise the brand but I caught a glimpse of the size: XL.

He still had to stretch it open with two thumbs.

Then came the chill of lube. Water-based and cold against my hot hole. But soon warmer and warmer as his masterful fingers smeared it around and inside. Preparing me for the burn we both knew was coming.

'Go slow,' I said.

'Absolutely.'

'Just to begin with.'

He nodded. Bent over me again. Lifted my arms and placed them around his neck. Slid his left hand, palm-up, under my back and between my shoulder blades and higher. Wrapped his fingers around my neck. Tight but not uncomfortable. Supported me and himself.

Then he kissed me.

Once. Twice. And on the third time he reached down with his free hand. Positioned the head of his cock against my hole as our lips touched. Pushed his tongue inside my mouth and let gravity and his body weight do the rest.

Pain seared through me fast like lightening. Striking hot but not unbearable. There was enough pleasure racing through my body, and excitement electrifying the air, to balance it out.

Closing my eyes, I forced myself to relax. Moaned into the darkness as he inched further inside, stretching me wider than any man or toy before him.

'Open your eyes,' he said gently, squeezing my neck and reaching his other hand to my arse, pulling my cheeks open wider.

I did as I was told. Opened my eyes slowly. Stared at him on top of me. Covering me completely. My jaw hanging an inch. My breath coming in short, sharp bursts.

'Beautiful,' he said, pushing further.

The pain kept coming. It rippled through me like a wave. Not crashing violently, but ebbing and flowing. Within ten seconds, I was lost in his deep, dark eyes and the weight of his body and the slow, steady rhythm of his gentle thrusts. Then the pain disappeared, morphing into a body-shuddering, eye-rolling ecstasy.

He saw it, plastered across my face. No more wincing. Big smile. Then he shifted his position a little. A slight but expert movement. He pulled himself up, towards the headboard, while simultaneously rolling his hips and pulling out of me to the tip.

At the same time, keeping one arm wrapped around his thick neck, I reached down and around his body. Traced the two ridges of hard muscle down his back to his arse. Placed my hand on a superb cheek. Gave it a quick squeeze and pulled him towards me, just as he rolled his body and thrusted back.

All the way to the base.

My body convulsed under him. My legs shook. My toes curled. My hole clamped tight, squeezing a moan out of his throat and filling my cock with so much blood, for a second, I thought I was going to unload hands-free. Then we kissed, hard and deep and passionately, as he held himself inside. Grinding his body against mine to ensure every inch of him was covered.

'Good boy,' he said, sliding back out and in again. 'Very good boy.'

I wanted to thank him. Thank sir for being so good to me. But I couldn't speak. My words weren't working. My brain was too busy being flooded with dopamine. So I nodded wildly instead. Gestured with my mouth and tongue for a kiss. Got what I wanted.

We kept kissing while he built his rhythm. And not just any wham-bam-in-and-out. Mr. Price was building the perfect rhythm with the perfect beat on the perfect instrument. His body, his bed and an outstanding balance of weight, force and timing. As he thrust he held me so my own body rocked back and forth. Back as he pulled out. Forth as he pushed in.

Phenomenal.

Then he increased speed. Slowly but surely. Faster and faster until he was fucking me just quicker than one full movement a second. His body slamming against me. Skin slapping against skin. The tempo held, kept steady like a philharmonic conductor.

Devoted to his craft.

He showed no signs of tiring or slowing down. None. Just kept going with eyes glued on mine. His breath controlled and even, heating my face as his sheets caressed my back. His hands now wrapped around the sides of my head. Beads of sweat glistening across his forehead under the moody light above us.

I watched them form. Fascinated. Wanted them to drip onto me. Onto my face and into my mouth so I could taste more of him.

It wasn't until we were both groaning loudly into the room around us did he have to catch his breath.

'Wow,' I said, catching my own. 'I'm so close.'

He smirked.

'Too soon,' he said, placing his hands on the back of my knees and pushing himself up to kneeling.

He looked down at the sight in front of him. I couldn't see but I could imagine what he saw. His cock, long and thick and hard and still inside my hairless, tight arse.

'Let's change position,' he said.

Pulling out the final few inches, he let go of my legs and wiped his face with his forearm. Took hold of my ankle and flipped me over onto my front, but kept me a little twisted so I could look back. One knee up by my chest, the other down the bed. Him still kneeling.

I bit my lower lip as he slid back in. Then he placed both of his hands on my hip. Pulled me into him as he pushed. Deep and intense. Over and over against my prostate, slow and controlled but brutal.

Then came doggy. First him kneeling behind me on the mattress. Still slow and controlled. Me taking the reins: bouncing myself up and down as he rested. Hands on his waist, sweat dripping off him and onto my back and arse. Then he pulled out again. Yanked me down the bed. Stood. Continued. Faster and harder until he folded over, panting and gasping for breath.

And believe me, that took a long time.

We were back to our original position when we were ready. Neither of us spoke but we could feel it. See it. Sense it in each other. His rhythm was on point. His thrusts were deep. Our eyes were locked and our breath and moans and grunts were in harmony.

Throwing his head back, he took in a sharp breath. Moaned, but not drawn out. Quick and uncontrollable. Then again. And again. Signs as clear as day.

Lulling my own rocking head back onto the pillow I looked down, over my nose, to his face. His mouth was wide open. His breath was fast. Our bodies were shaking and trembling as his endless beat pounded.

Faster and faster and faster.

Taking hold of myself I jerked off. Same speed. Same acceleration. But my balls were already filling and contracting, seconds away from emptying their cargo. It was still too soon. I wanted us to cum together.

I let go. Threw my arms around his neck. Pulled him in. Thrust my tongue into his open mouth.

No good. I'd already crossed the point of no return and my load was on its way.

Luckily, so was his.

'I'm going to cum,' he groaned, millimetres from my mouth; our foreheads crushed tight up against each other, hot and slippery but fixed in place like a bridge between our bodies.

'Me too.'

'Good boy. Good boy!'

My fingers dug into his shoulders. His huge arms held us both up. Then we came. Him inside me, filling the latex bubble so full I could feel it. Me all over my stomach and up to my nipples. Finally blasting out, no hands, like a geyser.

He stayed inside for a long time. Panting and dripping and kissing my mouth and neck and head. When we finally separated he balled up the condom in some tissue. Placed it on his bedside table, rolled back and spooned me.

Him big. Me small. Our sweat gluing us together.
Everything blissful. Everything beautiful. Everything
different than before.
    Until I opened my big fucking mouth.

Twenty-two

'What shall we do now?' I said.

'That's up to you,' he said, stroking a stray stand of my hair back into place.

His fingertips were hot against my forehead and a tingle spread out and around to the back of my head as he stroked. Then it blissfully rolled down my spine all the way to the soles of my feet.

Our spoon session over, he was on top of me again. In between my legs like before. Both of us still naked on his oversized bed; our cocks soft but our muscled bodies hard. His abs on mine. His chest on mine. My load dry and crusting on my stomach and sticking his chest hair together. Our breath slow and controlled and normal.

Everything else far from it.

'Oh yeah?' I said, lost in his sensual eyes.

'Yeah. The way I see it, you have two options,' he said.

'I like a choice.'

'One, we shower and I take you home. Or two, you stay here a little longer and we make more memories.'

'What time is it?' I said.

Shifting onto his side he peered at a small digital clock on his bedside table. Rolled back on top of me and said, 'Eleven.'

'Plenty of time,' I said.

'For?'

'Option two.'

'Good lad,' he said.

He kissed me on the mouth. Not fast but not slow either. Just the right amount of speed and force and softness and tongue.

Perfect.

Everything about him was. His body. His lips. His chin. His nose. His ears. His voice. His laugh. His cock.

His power.

I wanted more. I wanted to see what else I could add to the list of what was perfect about Mr. Price.

'I want to fuck you this time,' I said, my balls tightening at the thought of burying my cock between his cheeks.

But he laughed. Raised a single eyebrow and said, 'Don't hate me, but I'm not into that.'

I should have kept my mouth shut.

'Bullshit,' I said.

'Sorry, matey. It's not.'

I wasn't thinking straight. I was too caught up in the moment. Too excited. Too eager. Too idiotic.

'Yes, it is. You were on your back when your wife caught you,' I said.

Playtime over.

His smile vanished. His forehead crinkled and he cocked his head to the side. But not like before. Not smirking like in the park. Not sizzling with excitement like downstairs in the hallway. This time he was confused.

Confused and angry.

It was then I realised what I'd said. What I'd done. He'd told me about his wife. How she'd caught him with another man in the very room we were lying in. But he hadn't given me the details. The other man had given me those.

'Who told you that?' he said.

'You did,' I lied.

He rolled off me. All the way this time. Then he walked to the centre of the room and picked up his underwear. Pulled them on and up and turned. Stared at me for a second before moving to the end of the bed, blocking out the light from above.

In the darkness, his face was partially hidden, but I could still make out the whites of his eyes glistening in the dim. No, not glistening. Piercing into me like razor sharp icicles.

'No, I didn't,' he said.

'Yes, you did,' I lied again, sitting up against the headboard and looking around the room for my clothes as nonchalantly as I could. Panic rising in my throat.

I'd put my foot it in royally, and the only solution I could think of was to leave.

Get the fuck out.

But there was no sign. No sign of my shirt. No sign of my shorts. Underwear. Socks. Trainers. House key.

Then I remembered. Half of my outfit was outside on the landing. The rest was crumpled in a heap downstairs, carelessly discarded in the heat of the moment. I was completely naked. Naked and defenceless and cornered.

'Don't lie to me. I know what I told you, and I didn't say a single word about how or in what way my wife caught me. How do you know this?'

'I must have made it up,' I said, hopping off the bed and walking towards the door.

He sidestepped in front of me. All six-foot-three of him. Muscled and toned and unmoveable.

'Where do you think you're going?' he said.

'To get my clothes.'

'Not until you answer me.'

'Get out of my way.'

'No.'

I had three options.

One was to kick him in the balls and run. Fling my leg up and peg it like the wind, snatching up clothes as I went. Which might work in the movies, but not in reality.

Tim was a big guy, literally trained in physical education. And he'd played rugby all his life. He knew how to dodge and defend himself against oncoming body parts. There was a ninety-nine percent chance he would block and have me down on the floor immobilised in next to no time, even angrier.

The second was to tell the truth. Admit that I'd lied to him. That I knew all about his wife and how she'd caught him.

But then he would wonder. Wonder what else was a lie. The flood gates would open. How I knew where he ran. How old I was. Who told me I knew he was gay.

He would never trust me again, which would have been fine if he was some random hook-up. I would never see or think of him again. I wouldn't care. But he wasn't and I did. Mr. Price was the best I'd ever had and everything I'd always wanted. And I wanted him again.

Again and again and again.

Option two was no good. Not in a million years, which left option three. Keep lying and lie some more. Put the blame on someone else. Create a distraction so big it blindsided him from the truth.

Make someone else the problem.

'Ok. Ok. I'm sorry,' I said backing off. 'I shouldn't have lied to you, but I didn't even think it was true.'

'Explain yourself.'

Sitting on the side of the bed I hung my head. Bunched up my body into my shoulders. Made myself look ashamed and upset.

It worked. I sensed his body relax. His muscles unclench. His fists untighten.

'Adam Stanmore,' I said.

I didn't need to look up to know the name had made him flinch. At least mentally. But I did anyway.

Staring at the floor he slumped his shoulders. His eyes glazed over, lost in deep thought. No doubt thinking of the schoolboy he'd spent hours with on the pitch. In the changing room. In his car. His home. His bed.

The schoolboy who had made his life come crashing down like a tonne of bricks.

'I heard from some friends still at school that he came in a couple weeks ago,' I said. 'Fucked up. All battered and bruised.'

'Oh.'

'Yeah. They said his dad beat him up because he's gay or bi or whatever. Either way he doesn't seem to care who knows.'

'Fuck,' he muttered.

Like he was muttering to himself. Like he'd forgotten I was in the room with him. Then he looked down into my eyes for the first time in two minutes.

'Go on,' he said.

'We're not friends or anything. I mean, I was in the year above,' I lied. 'But I wanted to talk to him.'

'Why? So you could find out his secrets?'

197

'No. Nothing like that. I wanted to see if there was anything I could do. Because I know what it feels like. To get the shit kicked out of you for being different.'

He said nothing. Nodded. Then he sat next to me on the side of the bed. Not touching but close. Close enough to feel his heat and smell his body.

'I waited for him after school by the gates,' I said. 'To ask if there was anything I could do. But he told me he didn't need my help. He laughed in my face. Said his boyfriend would look after him.'

'He has a boyfriend?'

'Yeah,' I said, throwing Tim a look.

A look he deciphered instantly.

'He's saying I'm his boyfriend?' he said.

'Not to everyone. Or at least I don't think he is. But he did to me. It was like he was showing off. Bragging about bagging the ex-teacher. Just like he brags about fucking girls at his house parties.'

Tim's features softened and he nodded again. He was saying nothing but believing every word. But I couldn't lay off. I needed to finish the lie. Plant it deep and cement it over.

'I told him I didn't believe him. That he didn't need to make up stories to make himself feel better, because I didn't care who he stuck his dick in. But then he told me you and him had been fooling around since he was sixteen. He said he was the reason your wife left. He said he had you on your back when she came home.'

'He told you that?'

I nodded.

'And you believed him?'

'Like I said, not at first. I guessed you two must have spent a lot of time with each other, what with rugby

198

practice, but the idea that you might like guys was, well, honestly it was too good to be true. But then when I saw you out running, I couldn't stop thinking about you,' I said, resting my fingers on his forearm.

My touch snapped him out of his daze. His eyes locked on mine. Kind again. But tinged with something else.

Fear.

It was time to seal the deal with the best possible solvent. A sprinkling of truth.

'What?' he said.

'You were right. I did fall over on purpose.'

'What? Why?'

'I didn't know how else to talk to you. I thought you were ignoring me all those times I waved and smiled because Adam was telling the truth. That you two were together and you weren't interested.'

'Why didn't you just say hi?'

'I was jealous.'

'We're not together. I haven't seen him in over a year.'

'I know that now. Well, I went ahead and assumed. But I like you. I've fancied you since I can remember. I thought you and me would never get together, so I ignored what Adam said. Passed it off as bullshit from the world's biggest bullshitter. But then, watching you run around that field in your red t-shirt and your tiny shorts, I had to find out for myself. I'm sorry I didn't tell you before. I thought it would be best if I just pretended like I didn't know anything.'

'Why?'

'Because you'd think I was sad. And desperate. I would.'

He didn't reply. Not for a while at least. But he did put his arm around me. Around my shoulders.

Then he pulled me into him and kissed me on the side of the head.

'Thank you for being honest, Oscar,' he said.

'I'm sorry for not telling you sooner.'

'It's ok. I understand. It's difficult.'

'Are you ok?' I said.

'I've been better.'

'Can I help?'

'Not really.'

'You sure?'

'Just promise me you won't say anything about this to anyone. I could get in a lot of trouble if people hear what he's saying.'

'He's eighteen now.'

'It doesn't matter. What we did was wrong. And at the end of the day it's his word against mine. He's the star rugby captain and I'm the disgraced ex-teacher. I don't like my odds.'

'So, it's true? He was the guy she caught you with?'

'Yes. But the rest isn't. I haven't seen or spoken to him since I quit.'

'I'm guessing that's the reason you're not into taking it up the arse?'

He nodded. Then he nudged me playfully. Said, 'It does look like a lot of fun though.'

I laughed. But nowhere near as hard as I'd wanted. Mr. Price had just bought my utter bollocks about Adam and I'd managed to save myself by the skin of my teeth. I would have cackled maniacally if I could.

Then the room went quiet and neither of us spoke for almost two minutes.

'Should I go?' I said.

'Probably,' he said.

'Can I see you again?'

'Yes. I'd like that.'

'When?'

'How about this weekend? I'll cook for you. You can let me know exactly how terrible I am in the kitchen.'

We laughed. Then ten minutes later we were dressed. Two minutes after that I was in his car.

The journey to my house took five minutes and we talked the whole way. Talked about how great the evening had been. In the woods. On his sofa. Against the wall. On the landing. In his bed. We talked about how funny it was that I'd thrown myself in front of him and how glad he was that I had.

He parked a few doors down from my house and placed his hand on my leg, the car interior light bright and blazing between us. Our reflections in the black glass of the windows. Total darkness outside.

'Oscar, I want to say thanks for tonight.'

'You really don't need to thank me.'

'I do. It was nice to have someone to speak to. All the stuff about Adam aside, until tonight I didn't know how nice it could be to just be myself with someone. Someone who doesn't judge me over my past. So, thank you.'

His words hit me. Hard and soft at the same time, like a sledgehammer made of marshmallow, right in the centre of my ribs.

Then something peculiar happened. Something I hadn't felt in a very long time. A swelling in my chest. In my heart. Warm and strong and powerful, heating and radiating through me. Pulling my lips into a smile I couldn't shake.

I like him.

Not just his body or his legs or the fantasy of Mr. Price. I really liked him.

'It was a pleasure, sir,' I said, still unable to shake my smile. 'Are you going to talk to Adam?'

'About what he's been saying?'

I nodded, my fingers, toes and bollocks crossed for the answer I needed.

'No. I thought about it, but at the end of the day, I don't want to dredge up long-dead feelings. He can say what he wants, he's obviously going through a tough time, but just as long as other people don't corroborate his story I'm sure I'll be fine.'

Phew.

'I understand,' I said.

'Just one thing, though,' he said.

'What?'

'Is there anything else I should know? Anything else you're not telling me?'

'Like what?'

'Nothing specific. It's just, not so long ago, there were a lot of lies in my life. And I don't want that anymore. If something you've told me isn't true, no matter what it is, this is your chance to tell me. I won't care, I promise.'

My smile disappeared.

I thought about sitting on Adam's bed all those weeks ago. Listening to his stories and prying out the juicy information. Leaving him high and dry and then laughing in his face. Stalking Mr. Price. Watching him on my reconnaissance missions in the park. Waiting for the right time. Telling him I was nineteen. Pretending to know nothing about his past. Naked in his bed, with the hum of

202

his cock still resonating through my body, lying again and again.

Lost in his eyes, a small part of me wanted to tell the truth. The part buzzing and tingling from his words. *This is my chance. He won't care.*

Of course he will. I've been a psycho. If I tell him the truth, then what? It will be over and I'll never feel this feeling again.

'No,' I said. 'There's nothing else. I promise.'

'Good,' he said smiling. 'Sleep tight, handsome boy.'

'Good night, sir.'

What's the harm in one more lie?

More than I could have imagined.

Twenty-three

I slept like a log that night.

Smack, bang out of it and on my way to dreamland within a minute of face-planting my pillow. No shower. No wank. I didn't even check my phone.

All I could do was throw off my clothes, crawl under my duvet and let my final thoughts and feelings of the day play out through my exhausted mind and body like a movie reel stripped apart, cut up and reassembled at random.

The smell of Mr. Price on my skin. The buzz of my hole still tingling after its magnificent workout. The taste of beer and sweat on my tongue. The ache in my throat. The memory of his load, hot and gooey, spurting into my stomach. The sting of my knee after throwing myself in his path.

Trying to escape his bedroom. His interrogation. My brilliant lie. His car.

Then my mum.

Beautiful, like when I was a little kid. Not tired and stressed and sad like the last time I'd seen her.

Her long blonde hair, down to her shoulders, was almost shimmering in the sun streaming through a window behind her. Her grey-blue eyes the colour of ice but warm as summer. Her skin healthy and sun-kissed. Her lips full and smiling.

We were at home. Our home. In the kitchen. Dad was there too. Laughing at something he was reading in the paper.

Sat at the table he looked younger and fitter. His hair was thicker and his face was free of the ghostly wrinkles and lines I was used to seeing in the incessant blue glow of his computer screen.

He's happy.

They were excited about today. Something big was happening. Something to do with me.

'You can't be late, Oscar,' she said, pinning a gold flower to the lapel of a black blazer I realised I was wearing.

I looked down at myself. Under the blazer was a black shirt complete with gold tie and gold waistcoat. Below was a pair of black trousers that stopped above highly polished gold brogues.

'Your mother's right,' Dad said, placing his paper on the table and walking over to me.

He put his hands on my shoulders and beamed.

'It's your big day, son. You can't keep him waiting.'

Then there was a church.

Small and stone but with a steeple that reached to the sky. Long and thin like a needle it stretched on for miles, piercing a thick layer of grey ominous cloud and disappearing out of sight. So stretched it was distorted, like a glitch in a computer game. It shuddered and lurched and then suddenly disappeared, only to reappear exactly as it was half or a quarter-second later.

But no one seemed to notice.

Not one of the guests outside seemed to care. They were too busy looking at me. Standing still and staring. No smiles. No frowns. Blank, dead expressions on their faces.

Faces I don't recognise.

I tried to focus on a woman in a black dress and gold hat as I reached the church doors. Her eyes and nose and mouth moved like liquid. Anywhere I looked her features would slink out of sight.

Like water.

'Go on, son,' Mum said behind me, now dressed in black and gold. 'He's waiting for you.'

Taking a deep breath, I looked up. The steeple had disappeared. The sky was blue again and the sun was back out. The church was a normal size and shape. A fleeting bird song chirped through the air. Discordant and jarring.

'Hurry,' Dad said, his gold and black suit sharp and fitted.

I heaved open the heavy wooden doors but they flew open like they weighed nothing at all. Slamming against the walls inside they sent a deafening boom through the church.

A man, in a matching gold and black suit, was stood at an altar a long way away. Far longer than possible in such a small building, but the aisle, covered in a tatty, old red carpet, reached on regardless. He turned at the bang of ancient wood on ancient rock.

It was Tim. Too far away to see, but I knew it was him. Tim Price, waiting for me.

We're getting married?

I took a step forward. And another. Then another and another. But no matter how many I took I couldn't get any closer. No matter how far I walked he stayed out of reach. Waiting for me to join him.

Beckoning me closer.

I ran. As fast as I could. The carpet below whirring under my feet like a treadmill. The same fibres, the same brown stains and the same frayed edges repeating and repeating as my arms and legs pumped.

Then I tripped, forward onto my face, but as I hit the ground the floor disintegrated. It shattered apart like exploding glass. Benches and carpet and bibles and candles falling and spinning like Alice down the rabbit hole. Tumbling alongside me into darkness.

Until I landed. Abrupt but softly and upright in a chair. An old green, fabric chair in an office.

Mr. Price's office.

In front of me was his computer. On the computer was a folder. Nameless. I clicked it open and double clicked the single file inside.

It was a video. A video of Adam and Mr. Price standing in a bedroom and kissing.

Tim's bedroom.

Half-naked: their shirts off. Their hard, muscular torsos against each other. Their strong hands touching and gliding over bulging biceps and pecs and triceps and deltoids and abs.

Then the camera panned back. Lying on the bed, naked and smirking, was James.

My ginger pocket rocket, grinning up at them. Him five-foot-five and on his back. Mr. Price ten inches taller and Adam three inches taller still now either side of the bed. Dwarfing the smooth, toned teen like giants.

Then James sat up, got on all fours and opened his mouth. Began to work Adam's cock, sucking on it until he was as hard as diamond between his lips. Mr. Price moved to the other end. Pulled James's arse apart and ate his hole.

I watched. Astonished. Amazed. And then furious.

My stomach twisted as Tim's powerful jaw stopped moving. I shook with rage as he gathered a mouthful of spit and let it fly. Tears began to well as he slid himself inside raw.

For five seconds, I watched them fuck him. Roast James like a pig on a spit. Both staring at each other, grunting and moaning. Reaching out and caressing. Stroking. Pinching.

All three loving every second. James abandoning himself. Adam lost in Tim's eyes. Tim lost in his.

Tim. Lost.

Bleep, bleep, bleep! My alarm yanked me back to consciousness. Loud and fast and disorientating.

Clawing at my bedside table, I picked up my phone. Seven in the morning. Thumbing the alarm to snooze I snuggled back under the covers for warmth, my heart still pounding.

What the fuck was that? A nightmare?

But it shouldn't have been. The whole messed-up church scenario aside, the idea of Tim and Adam working James between the two of them was ball-tinglingly awesome. Especially if I had a ringside seat or a camera for action shots.

At least it should have been. Lying in bed, my forehead beading with sweat, all I could think about was how I'd felt. Upset. Envious. Scared.

Weak.

Picking up my phone again, I checked my texts. Four new messages. All from James from the night before. Each getting progressively more annoying and needy.

First, he'd asked if I was still coming over. Then if I was ok. Then if there'd been a reason why I was ignoring

208

him. Then, finally, one last instalment calling me a dickhead. All from not coming over one evening out of too many to count.

This kid isn't worth the trouble.

Throwing my phone at a pile of dirty clothes on the floor, I rolled out of bed and made my way to the bathroom.

I used the toilet and showered. Brushed my teeth and did my hair. Back in my room I dressed in my uniform. White shirt, navy blue blazer, black trousers, purple and navy striped tie. Black socks and shoes.

Dad's door was closed, as usual, but there were no sounds of mouse clicks or keyboards being furiously tapped. No swearing through headphones at spotty teenagers on the other side of the world.

Maybe he's actually gone to sleep.

Down in the kitchen I put two slices of bread under the grill and made a cup of tea. Sat and sipped, still digesting my dream, as my breakfast slowly crisped under red hot elements.

There was only one explanation. One explanation to why I'd gotten upset. Why seeing the three of them together had made my blood boil and why I'd dreamt about marrying the guy.

I really like him.

More than his body. More than using him to escape my cesspit of a home and school life. I missed him.

His voice, his smell, his touch.

I didn't want to marry him. Marriage was something my parents did, so naturally I'd decided years ago that there was no way I would ever tie myself to another person like that. Tie myself to their life and their problems until death do us part.

Not in a million years.

But it must have meant something. Something big.

Not to mention the fact that, as I spread butter and jam onto my toast, when it came to James and his texts waiting unanswered in my inbox, I didn't care.

I didn't give a toss if he didn't want to see or speak to me again. After all my hard work grooming and preparing him to get double dicked, he didn't matter anymore. All that time wasted and I wasn't bothered. I wasn't even that bothered about seeing Adam again.

It's all about Pricey.

I thought about him on the walk to school and all through first and second periods. French and music. Thought about him at break. Fantasised about him so much during double English I had to spend fifteen minutes in the library toilets at lunch rubbing one out.

But as I stepped back into the cold, red-faced and semi-hard under my school trousers, my pondering on what the two of us were going to get up to on the weekend was cut short. Literally.

James. We collided. His face, my chest.

'Sorry,' he muttered, scurrying backwards and out of my way, no doubt an inbuilt response for a short arse like him.

But then he looked up and his demeanour shifted in an instant. Submissive subservience to narrow-eyed fury.

'Oh. It's *you*,' he said.

For a moment, I contemplated rolling my eyes and ignoring him. Walking away from his bitching. But, with the endorphins from freshly emptied balls still surging, I was prepared to hear him out. Humour him for a few minutes.

210

After all, as much as I had bigger fish to fry, his arse was still one of the best I'd ever had. So, I decided that I should try to kill two birds with one stone. Set him straight and sweet talk him back to my side.

'Well spotted,' I said.

'Where the fuck *were* you last night? You said you were coming over.'

'Yeah sorry, something came up.'

'Why didn't you text me?'

'I forgot.'

'You forgot?'

'Listen, James,' I said, taking him by the arm and pulling him around the corner, away from a passing group of year tens. 'What's your problem?'

'My problem?'

'Yeah, your problem. Why do you have to text me twenty-four seven?'

'I don't text you twenty-four seven!'

'Surely you get my point, though? I'm still at the same school as you. I still live in the same town.' Checking left and right – all clear – I ran the backs of my fingers down his cheek. 'I'm not going anywhere.'

He moved his head away, but looked up through calmer eyes. He frowned.

'I just don't understand why you didn't reply.'

'Like I said, I'm sorry, I forgot.'

'Do you even want to be my boyfriend?'

I'd been waiting for that question for days. Maybe even a week. It had been clear for a long time he thought we were dating. Officially together and all that bollocks. There'd just been no need to break his delusion.

Until now.

Taking a deep breath I collected my thoughts. It was earlier than I'd wanted, but it was now or never. Placing my hands either side of his waist, I pulled him in close.

'Listen, handsome. I need to tell you something,' I said.

'What?' he said, his nervous eyes darting left and right, trying to read mine.

Nervous because of what I was doing and where we were, but also the same nerves as the first time I'd ever touched him. Scared but loving it.

'This boyfriend thing. I'm super flattered, but I have to be honest with you. I don't think I can do it.'

His eyes widened in sadness and shock. He pulled away from my hold. His mouth opened a fraction, saying nothing.

'But it's not you. It's me. I promise,' I continued.

'So what? That's it? You're just going to stop talking to me all of a sudden?'

'No, no. Not at all. What I mean is, I can't be your boyfriend because it wouldn't be fair on you.'

'Fair?'

'Yeah. Fair. I'm not ready for it. I want more.'

'What do you mean more?'

'Adam.'

'Adam?'

'He wants to join in. With us. And I want it too.'

'Join in?'

'A threesome. You, me, him.'

'I get the picture!' he snapped.

'Come on, don't tell me you're not keen on the idea?'

'All this time,' he said, his eyes glistening with tears. 'All this time when you talked about him. About how

212

he wanted to get together so he could have someone to relate to. That was all crap, wasn't it? You've never cared about me. You were just using me.'

'That's not true,' I said.

But it didn't sound convincing. I was already switching off and it was beginning to show. He shook his head. Wiped his eyes. Then he began to walk away.

'Come on, James. Don't be a pussy. You'll love it,' I said, no more shits to give.

It didn't go down well.

'Fuck you, Oscar.'

After that, other than in class or across the field or in the corridor, I didn't see James again. But like I said, I didn't care.

I have Tim.

Twenty-four

The rest of the school day was uneventful.

Other than my tedious, but thankfully brief altercation with James, lunch ended without a hitch. There were the usual looks when I walked past a group of lads or unzipped at the urinals to take a piss, but there were no problems.

No jeers. No name-calling. No pushing or shoving or tripping or spitting. In fact, as the bell rang, loud and shrill through the old, stone corridors and grey, concrete quads, and I took a seat at the back of my next class, I realised I hadn't had any real trouble for days.

Ever since Adam had turned up that Wednesday morning black and blue I'd been relatively left alone. Ever since their king had suddenly become an almighty batty-boy, something had changed. The dynamic had shifted. His pathetic followers were confused. Unsure on best bullying etiquette.

I could see it in their eyes.

I could see their measly brains trying to process me. Their gut reaction to shout or throw something, followed a split-second later by a thought. A memory. A recollection that their mate, their big, rugby-captain pal Adam was a queer, fudge-packing, shirt-lifting cock-sucker too.

And that six-foot-six cock-sucker had made it clear he wasn't going to take it lying down.

It had happened a couple days after he'd come back to school; his bruises and cuts already fading. Unsurprisingly a beta male, pumped with hormones and cheap energy drinks, had taken his chance. Attempted to dethrone the weakened alpha while the going had been good.

Or, in his case, not so good.

I hadn't seen it. Sadly. I'd learned a long time ago it was in my best interest to avoid large groups, but I'd overheard the glorious chatter in the lunch line the following week.

Rumour had it that Adam had been walking across the field to the sports hall and a group of lads had cut him off. Mainly boys from the football team, but one or two from the second rugby team. Including a six-foot-two, acne-ridden reprobate called Rory Saunders.

Saunders had done the usual. Squared up to him. Got up in his face. Started saying all the typical stuff like how faggots weren't wanted in this school and how they had no place on sports teams. But then he'd got personal. Said Adam only played rugby so he could look at the boys in the changing rooms. Called him a pervert.

Big mistake.

Next thing you know Rory's rolling on the ground with an imploded nose. Crushed almost flat by Adam's forehead and gushing blood and bits of pulverised cartilage and bone.

After that, as far as I could tell (and bar a week of detention: they'd gone easy on him considering his "situation"), everything had gone back to normal for Adam.

Back at the top of the food chain. Still rugby captain. Still loved and admired and feared across the school like I'd said he would in the staff car park on his first day back.

But I'd also been wrong that afternoon. What I hadn't appreciated until now, so far distracted by my quest for the holy grail that was Mr. Price and his heavenly legs, was that things had changed.

For me.

I was still far from accepted – I was a full-blown bender whereas Adam was only half an abomination – but it was beginning to look like what he'd offered was coming to fruition. That I didn't need to watch my back anymore.

I could actually listen to my iPod, not keep it muted to hear footsteps racing up behind me. I could pass the playing field without the fear of a football or a can of Coke to the face. And, for the first time in a long time, I could answer a question in class without people sniggering or making lame innuendos or tired, boring jokes.

'Very good, Oscar. Correct. It's nice to hear you speak. Do it more, please,' the teacher said, turning back to the whiteboard before scribbling my response in large, slanted green letters.

Enjoying the rare swell of academic pride in my chest I smiled to myself. Pulled out my phone from my trouser pocket and unlocked it under my desk. I had about two minutes to talk to Adam while Mrs. Burton explained the difference between fact and inference to the rest of the class, her attention now successfully deflected away from me.

> **Hey. I've got an update on our little mate. Can we meet?**

Forty seconds later his reply vibrated in my hand.

After school. Same place as last time.

Two hours later it was me waiting for him. Leaning against the red brick of the art block that made up one border of the staff car park, hidden by the shadows of the oak tree and the fast-creeping darkness of the autumn afternoon.

It was cold. The coldest day of the year so far. I cursed myself for not bringing a jumper, too busy thinking about Tim and my weird dream to think about much else that morning, as I breathed clouds of billowing steam around my hands and willed blood to flow faster around my fingers.

Small stones below me crunched as I hopped and stepped from side to side. The earthy scent of wet, muddy grass blanketing the adjacent field chilling my nostrils.

Seven minutes in, I considered calling him, but as I reached for my phone he turned the corner. Tall and broad and beautiful in his school uniform. His rugby captain's tie and a thick, burgundy scarf wrapped around his neck. His limp gone and his black eye now a light brown. Barely even noticeable in the fading light.

We'd been texting almost every day, about James, about what we were going to do to him if I ever managed to convince him to open his legs for both of us, but we hadn't seen each other. Not properly. Not face-to-face.

He looked almost as good as new. Maybe even better.

'You look good,' I said, ceasing my two-step and forcing my teeth to stop chattering. 'They let you back in the gym?'

'Yeah,' he said, leaning against the wall about a metre from me. He looked away.

'I heard about what happened with Rory Saunders.'

He said nothing. Just turned his neck to look at me; his eyes as cold as the air itself. Then he raised his eyebrows and nodded. Looked away again.

'That dickhead got what he deserved,' I said.

'Whatever. What do you want?'

'Alright, chill out. What's your problem?'

He looked at me and stared. Hard. Then said, 'Nothing. It's fucking freezing and I'm tired. I want to go home.'

I scanned him up and down. He did look tired. And cold.

'Fair enough. I'll make this quick,' I said. 'James is a no-go.'

'What? Why?'

'Long story short he's not as stupid as I thought.'

'What do you mean?'

'When I tried to bring you up, in a more direct sense, he saw straight through me. Seems he wants me all to himself or not at all. I doubt I'll be seeing him again.'

He shook his head and said, 'Sloppy.'

'Excuse me?'

'You had him practically eating out of your hand and now he's gone? Sounds sloppy to me.'

'Ok. Fuck you.'

'Am I wrong?'

The annoying thing was he wasn't. Probably for the first time in his life the dim-witted slab of muscle was right. I had been sloppy. I could have easily saved the situation if I'd tried harder. But I hadn't.

218

And I definitely don't need Adam Stanmore pointing it out.

'Yeah. You are,' I lied. 'I wasn't sloppy. I was too busy getting fucked by Mr. Price last night to give a shit about that whiney bitch.'

I watched his face as my words left my mouth. Waited for them to hit and sink in. Waited to see his lips or eyes droop or his forehead to wrinkle. His shoulders to slump or his nostrils to flare. I wanted to see the pain written across his face.

But it didn't come. He smiled. Then he laughed.

'It's true,' I said, trying my best to hide the confusion creeping across my own.

'I'm sure it is,' he said, still smiling. 'I hope the two of you are very happy together.'

'What's that supposed to mean?'

'Nothing. Like I said, I hope you're happy.'

Then neither of us spoke. Him staring, the same smirk across his obnoxious but still handsome face. Me trying to figure out what was going on. Why he hadn't even batted an eyelid when I'd told him about Tim.

Then it hit me. It was obvious. He didn't believe me. Plain and simple. Otherwise there was no *way* he would have reacted like that. Cool and calm and uncaring.

Yes, he'd told me, stood in this exact location, that he was done with Mr. Price. But I remembered that Sunday morning in his parents' bedroom vividly. I remembered his face. His eyes. Sad and confused and lonely. Wondering if he would ever see his first love again. If he would ever speak to him. Look at him. Touch him.

There's no way he's happy for me.

'Believe what you like,' I said. 'It's the truth.'

'Whatever,' he said. 'Is that it?'

'Is what it?'

'Is that all you wanted to talk about?'

I considered thanking him. Mentioning my life at school had improved since he'd come out as bi. That, amazingly, it was somehow safer for me now. But there was something in his smile and in his stare. They were more than simple façades: cover-ups of his jealousy and insecurities. There was something else in there.

Contempt.

Fuck him. I would rather eat my own shit and die of dysentery than thank him now.

'Yeah that's everything,' I said.

As I spoke, a set of headlights turned into the car park. A BMW, charcoal in the evening twilight, but flashing brilliant silver as it passed under the school floodlights.

'It's a shame, Oscar,' he said, pushing himself off the wall. 'I was really hoping you were about to tell me we would have some fun with that lad tonight.'

'Why tonight?'

'No reason,' he said, his smile widening.

Walking over to the car he opened the passenger door. Scoffed to himself again and then shot me a look. But he wasn't hiding anything anymore. It was a look dripping with disdain and hatred.

A look designed not just to kill, but to hang, draw, quarter and then set my disembowelled corpse ablaze.

'Have a good weekend,' he said.

Slam.

The car drove away. I watched it turn left out the car park and join the rest of the meandering traffic, almost ethereal among the red and yellow clouds of exhaust smoke and steam.

Thoughts flew around and around my head as I walked home.

Adam was undoubtedly upset about Mr. Price. That was obvious enough, going by his farewell. But tough shit. I'd already told him I was after Pricey and he'd given me the go ahead. Not that I'd even needed it.

If he was going to let his hopeless, long-expired feelings get in the way of any chance of fun between us in the future, then that was his problem. If he wanted to sulk and stew, then he could be my guest. I didn't need him anymore.

But there was something about what he'd said to me that stuck. Anchored itself in the pit of my stomach and began to bubble and churn as I crossed the field toward my house.

Have a good weekend.

He was planning something.

He knew where Tim lived. He knew about us. It was safe to assume Tim and I would be seeing each other again, so maybe he was going to make a surprise appearance? Confess his undying love. Tell Mr. Price the truth. Expose my lie.

Which cannot happen.

Luckily it was easily avoidable. I'd just have to convince Tim to take us somewhere else. Somewhere out of town. To a hotel in the city maybe. A dirty weekend.

Problem solved.

If only I'd known the problem was just beginning.

Twenty-five

The moment I made it home, I dumped my bag on the floor, pulled off my blazer and yanked off my tie.

Undoing the top two buttons of my white school shirt I threw myself onto my bed. Landed on the fading duvet on my stomach, bundled a pillow under my chest and propped myself up on my elbows so I could get at my phone. Successfully retrieved I unlocked it and reread Tim's most recent message to me.

Can't wait until Saturday sexy. We're gonna have so much fun.

The tingle in my body every time I thought about him warmed through me.

His tingle.

A tingle made of memories. Memories of the park and his kitchen and his living room and his bedroom and his car swirling in my head and through my veins. I smiled to myself, still not really believing I was going to see him again so soon.

Saturday is tomorrow.

I thumbed out a message.

Evening handsome. I have an amazing idea.
Tomorrow, how about we jump in your car and go somewhere? We could find a nice place to stay and really

222

Satisfied with ensuring a peaceful weekend away from whatever sad surprise Adam had in store, even though I'd told myself not to message until the morning, until at least twenty-four hours had passed to keep Tim keen, I put my phone away. Coming across a touch less smooth was an ok price to pay if it meant saving my skin.

I rolled onto my back.

My bedroom ceiling was disgusting. I stared at it for at least three minutes. Traced the large brown damp patch staining the greying white paint. Listened to the incessant tick-tock of the clock in the hallway as I searched for the starting point. Where the rot had set and grown and spread.

A car honked somewhere outside, snapping me out of my stupor. The blare came from at least the next street over, but it was still audible through the thin sheet of glass that did nothing to keep the growing winter at bay. My windows hadn't received the double-glazed treatment my Dad's had.

I shook my head. Fast.

Getting stuck in a mental black hole over my miserable excuse for a father and this house I was meant to call home was a bad idea. I couldn't let the excitement of tomorrow be overshadowed by the hopelessness of everything else. I had to be productive.

I have time to kill.

Rocking up to sitting, I swivelled on my arse and stood. Headed downstairs. Dad's door was closed as per usual; the tap-tap-click of his computer games drumming quietly into the narrow hallway. The peeling wallpaper by the bathroom door worse than this morning.

Taking the stairs two at a time, I reached the kitchen and opened the cupboard. Pulled out a jar of instant coffee and flicked on the kettle. Grabbed a mug. One sugar, a teaspoon of freeze-dried caffeine and a splash of milk from the fridge.

Dinner.

I had contemplated eating. But there was nothing that resembled food in the house other than the greasy, empty polystyrene trays of Dad's dinner. Chinese today. Sweet and sour chicken judging by the red, sticky, congealed stain on the counter.

I'd been meaning to go to the shops for days. But with James and Adam and Mr. Price keeping me occupied I'd relied on school lunches to see me through.

The trip would do me good, I thought, as long as I kept my head down and stayed clear of large groups of hoodie-wearing lads. *To pass the time, if anything.*

But as the tinkle of my teaspoon rattled inside my mug, I made up my mind.

No. No meal tonight.

I didn't want an inch of fat on my body tomorrow. I wanted every muscle and every line to be ripped and defined. Every inch of me as perfect as possible. Kissable. Lickable.

And fuckable. The best kind of fuckable, which meant being empty. Completely cleaned out.

Not that I minded douching. It was simple when you got the hang of it. I just knew first-hand the difference between a slick, flushed-out arse and the tight, grittiness of a more natural-feeling hole. The former was great, always, but if there were no unpleasant surprises the latter won hands down.

And Pricey deserves the best.

224

Making my way back upstairs I sipped the sweet, steaming liquid. Hotness dripped through me, down my throat, and my balls pulsed so hard I almost scolded myself.

The coffee had felt like his load. Tim's load, spurting into my stomach like it had done two nights ago; my hands tied behind my back; his fat cock wedged down my neck.

Steadying myself against the wall, I enjoyed the aches of my groin as my swelling cock grew inside my underwear. Reaching my room, I placed my mug on my desk and threw myself onto my bed.

I was rock hard. My cock stretching thick and long under black polyester school trousers and white cotton briefs all the way across my right leg.

I wanted to jerk off so badly. Wrap my fingers around myself and squeeze and tug. It had felt like I could still feel him. Inside my mouth. My jaw still aching. My tongue still squashed down. His powerful hands still gripping my head.

I could still hear him. His grunts and moans. Still smell him. His sweat. His load whipped up with my saliva, streaming out of my nostrils as he'd pulled out. Salty like sea air.

But, again, no. *Save it.*

Beating off was never the same as the real thing, and I was sure Tim would appreciate a full pair of balls. He might not have been into bottoming, but from the way he'd licked up my load from my chest, I was certain he would happily enjoy a mouthful.

Don't want to let him down with only one day of build-up.

I checked my phone. No response yet, which was fine. He was probably out running. It was Friday. He ran on Fridays.

Turning my head, I looked at my slanted, upside down reflection in the wardrobe mirror across from my bed. Curved my body like a cat so I could see my chest and stomach and legs. Undid all the buttons on my shirt and pulled it open. Looked at my abs and V-lines. At my pecs.

Standing I shrugged off my shirt and unbuttoned my trousers. Pulled the zip slowly, pretending I was stood in front of Tim. Imagined I was him and my reflection was me. Grinned like I hoped he would at my bulge slowly showing thicker and thicker as the tiny metal teeth came apart. Then my trousers fell to my ankles, showing off my white briefs clinging tight and full around my thighs.

Stepping out of the crumpled black I turned around. But not fully. Just enough so I could see my arse and my back and the backs of my legs.

Not bad. Not bad at all. But there's always room for improvement.

Taking a large gulp of coffee, I turned on my computer. It had been my dad's before he'd needed a new one for his games. It was so battered no one had wanted to buy it, so he'd begrudgingly given it to me. It had iTunes.

I pressed play on my running playlist and pop music blared into my room. I had no idea who the artist or band was. I hadn't cared when I'd pressed download.

Just as long as it makes me sweat.

Grabbing a towel, I laid it on the floor between my bed and the mirror. Peeled off my socks, took another hot gulp of energy and laid on my back on the clean, scratchy white fabric.

Turning my head toward the mirror, I ran a hand down my stomach one more time. Watched myself in the glass as the hard ridges of my six-pack brushed under my palm.

Sit-ups first.

One-hundred-and-fifty in total. Ten sets of fifteen. Each time visualising Mr. Price holding my feet against the floor, like he'd used to, kneeling in front of the boys on the school rugby pitch.

With each rep, I got closer and closer to his stunning eyes and thick, model's lips. Closer to his pecs and his bulging biceps and triceps and deltoids. Beads of sweat rolling down my forehead and cheeks and chest.

Then I flipped over. Wiped my wet, red face on the towel and did the same number of push-ups. This time imagining him somewhere just as inspiring.

Exhausted, I flopped onto my back and looked at the ceiling again. Made my vision blur, like I was looking through the neglect, and concentrated on my breathing instead. Back to normal, I stood up and picked up my phone.

Still no text.

But still ok. I'd only spent thirty or so minutes exercising. A run, if you factor getting to and from the house, as well as showering, can often take an hour. Maybe two depending on how far you go. How far you push yourself. And Tim was fit.

Shrugging, I scooped up the towel from the floor, wrapped it around my waist and walked to the bathroom. Dad's door was open and his room was empty; I could hear him rattling around downstairs.

Glass chinked against wood. Twice: a tumbler and a bottle. Jack Daniels.

A shower will help. Help take my mind off the wait. Tim would be finished by the time I was out.

Surely.

Twenty minutes later I was back in my room, washed and dried and in a pair of grey jogging bottoms, a tight white t-shirt and a navy-blue jumper. The heating was on, for once, so I didn't need to wrap myself in my duvet or add three extra layers. My breath wasn't even steaming.

But I still had no word from Tim. No message. No missed call.

Typing a text to my own number I hit send. Just to check. Four letters pinged into my room immediately.

TEST

My phone was working. I had signal. Maybe he was going to wait until he'd cooked himself dinner, I wondered. Settled down for the night. Or maybe he was contemplating where to take me. Trying to think of somewhere exciting for us to go.

Where the fuck is he?

He'd been good on the text front. So far. Better than good. He'd replied pretty much straight away every time. Tim was eager. A good eager. And he wasn't afraid to show it.

Why now?

Swallowing the unease rising in my chest, I took a seat at my desk and opened MSN on my computer. I realised, with James gone, now I had a chance to chat to all the other lads I'd been working on.

All the boys that had taken up my time until Adam had turned up the heat. All the boys questioning their sexuality. Wondering what it would be like to feel another

228

lad's cock in their mouth, or if fucking arse really was tighter.

Some I hadn't spoken to in weeks, which should have made me excited. Eager to start stirring the pots again. Start fanning the flames of all those hormone-ridden, testosterone factories. But I didn't.

The unease I'd swallowed wasn't disappearing. It was growing and building. Turning and twisting and rumbling like a gathering storm.

Something was wrong. With Tim. I pulled out my phone.

Hey, you ok? We still on for tomorrow?

I hit send. A minute passed. Five minutes passed. Nothing. No reply.

For hours, I tried to ignore it. Ignore the blank screen in my pocket and focus on the windows of text popping up on my computer instead. On the stories Dan and Phil and Jemal and Edward and Oliver were spinning. But I wasn't interested. They weren't the same.

They don't matter anymore.

Three hours after my second text, I finally cracked. Yanked my phone out of my pocket and opened my address book. Scrolled down to Tim Price and pressed call.

The dull hum of a ringtone droned into my ear.

Twenty-six

The phone rang.

Quiet and monotonous. A double-beat through the tiny speaker pressing against my ear. Two-trills of digital noise lasting less than a second each, but ominous. Ominous enough to make my heart beat hard.

Hard and loud and heavy.

It rang again and my palms grew sweaty; the rigid grey plastic of my phone turning slick and slippery. Tightening my grip, I rubbed my free hand against my joggers; blood pumping like a drum through the cartilage sandwiched between my head and the handset.

Three rings. I swapped hands. Four. My neck ached.

It already hurt. Strained and stretched by Mr Price shooting his hot, tangy bolt into my stomach. My hands tied behind my back. My skull and mouth his personal property to use as he'd wished.

But the ache was different. No longer was it a trophy or a reminder of our time together. Now, and so suddenly, it was becoming something bad. A painful reminder that, I didn't have him yet. A man who had made my wishes come true. Who had talked to me like an adult and had treated me like one.

It felt like he was lost to me for a reason I didn't know but was undeniably growing inside of my gut like tangled thorns.

Five rings. Six. Seven. Nothing. Nothing but the steady beat of an unanswered call in a void of sizzling white noise.

Where is he?!

Then my thumping heart pounded. His voice. It boomed through the quiet. Strong and manly and confident. I took a quick breath. Composed myself.

But my jaw hung in the air. My excitement plummeted, all the way to the floor. In its place, a sickening dread.

Voicemail.

'Hi, you've reached Tim Price. Sorry I can't get to the phone right now. Please leave a message after the tone and I'll get back to you as soon as I can.'

Hanging up before the beep, I threw my phone at my bed. It bounced off the springy top, hitting the wall by my window, before crashing noisily to the floor.

I didn't move. Even if I'd thrown it hard enough to break I didn't care. Unwanted questions and more pressing problems were elbowing their way in and stomping around my mind.

Why is he ignoring me? Where is he? Who is he with? What is he doing?

My heart sank.

Has Adam got to him already?

Possible, but improbable.

Why drop the bomb without all parties around to get obliterated? And judging by the look of pure hatred Adam had shot me, climbing into his mum's car, I doubted he would waste an opportunity to watch my face as he poured gasoline on my relationship with Tim and lit a match.

Not that I was going to let him get anywhere near us.

It was simpler, then. *It must be*. And there was nothing simpler than another person. Tim must have found someone else. Another twink to play with. Another boy to turn into a man.

James?

Standing from my computer chair, I took a deep breath to cool the flames of jealously licking at my chest and head. It didn't help. I took another and the flames grew, fanned by oxygen and uncertainty.

Striding across my room, I picked up my phone. It was fine. No scratches or marks. No dents. But no messages or returned calls.

Nothing.

Slumping onto my bed, I forced myself to ignore the crushing scenarios rolling around my head like boulders. Pushed aside the flashbacks of my dream that morning. Of Tim and Adam and James without me.

I busied myself by considering my options. It wasn't much of a distraction. I didn't have many.

I couldn't message him again. *Not a chance.* It would come across too desperate. Calling had been bad enough. But at least if he'd answered I could have pretended that I'd pocket-called him. Rang him by accident and then casually checked if we were still on for tomorrow. Laid and cemented and built on my pre-emptive strategy to get away from Adam.

But he hadn't answered. And now he had two messages and a missed call from me on his phone. Anything more, like a voicemail, would cross into James territory.

232

And if that happened, I'd be no better than the needy little boys I couldn't stand.

Other than turning up at his house and knocking on his front door like a madman, I had no choice but to wait it out. Wait out each agonising second. Try to channel the virtue I've always had trouble with.

Fuck you, patience.

I checked the time on my phone. Almost ten at night. Dad's muffled shouts at his computer screen resounded through the walls and into my room. Then the house went quiet again. Turning to my window, I opened the curtains and looked out.

Past the smeared glass and the dim reflection of my face, the sky was a mixture of vivid greys. Completely blanketed by thin cloud it was illuminated by the bright white moon somewhere behind. Below the inverse, night-time carpet the yellow tinged street was lit by two dim street lamps spaced ten or so metres apart.

Something in the corner of my eye darted toward one of the parked cars lining the closest pavement. Too small to be a cat. Too quick to be a dog.

A rat?

A bird. All alone and hidden if not for its shadow, its black silhouette stretching out from the camouflaged car bonnet and across the concrete like a Dali painting.

Go to his house.

No. I'd already decided, after he'd dropped me off the other night and asked if there was anything else I should tell him, that I wasn't going to do anything like that anymore. No more stalking and spying. It was too risky.

Too much at stake. Too much to lose.

But, I told myself I wouldn't knock on his door. I would watch. Stay invisible like my sly, feathered-friend down there. Keep quiet and keep an eye out for signs of Adam. Or James. Or anyone.

Or even nothing. Anything that showed me he wasn't home. That he was out and too busy to text me back. That everything was fine. That it was all in my head.

I looked at my bed. Told myself to forget about it. To go to sleep and wait until the morning. To calm the fuck down and sort myself out. But I couldn't. I couldn't quiet the voice in my head. My own voice. Cold and cruel and uncaring.

He's fucking someone else. I know he is. He never wanted me. He just wanted my body. That's all I'm good for. Two holes to dump a load in. As if I thought he would ever want me. Nobody wants me. Not Tim. Not Adam. Not James. Not even my parents.

'Shut up!' I shouted, wrenching open my wardrobe doors.

Three minutes later, I was ready. Dressed all in black. Black jeans, black t-shirt and a black sweater. Black trainers and black socks. Turning my phone to silent, I placed it in my pocket. Picked up my house keys from my desk.

But as my fingers wrapped around the cold metal of my bedroom door knob my leg vibrated. Twice, but quickly. A one-two buzz in rapid succession. A text.

From him.

Hey! Sorry for the radio silence, it's been a crazy day. Definitely still on for tomorrow and really like the idea of a hotel night. Naughty boy ;)

For a second, I couldn't believe my eyes; my poisonous inner-monologue silenced. Then came relief.

Fast and refreshing like a dam bursting. The weight of it all gushing and flowing and falling away.

It peeled off my shoulders like it had never been there. All the crazy ideas and terrible reasons evaporated like steam, warming my cheeks and turning them red. All the pain and fear of losing him now silly and stupid.

Letting out the longest sigh of relief of my life, I let myself fall backwards onto my bed. Beamed at the ceiling as I bounced and sunk into my mattress, kicking off my trainers. I began to laugh. At the absurdity of it all. At how scared and angry and foolish I'd been.

At how a man had made me feel.

But he wasn't just any man. He was my man. Tim fucking Price. A man who couldn't wait to see me. Who did want me. Who cared about me.

And I cared about him. I did.

For the first time since I was fourteen, I actually cared about someone else. I could feel it, like a hot water bottle against my chest. In the release still rushing through my bones and muscles. In the ache in my neck.

Lifting my phone up and in front of my face to block out the glare of my bedroom light, I unlocked it and opened my messages.

Hey! That's cool, no worries. And awesome, glad to hear it. What time should I come over? Or do you want to pick me up? :p

I hit send and within twenty seconds his reply buzzed into my hand. Fast and attentive like usual.

Come to mine and we'll go from there. 6pm?

I can come earlier if you like?

Ok. 4pm?

Perfect.

Great. You're going to get it.

Get what?

You'll see.

Come on. Give me a taste.

Ok. I want you on your stomach. Back arched. Arse in the air. Your hole smooth and hairless.

Done. I want you to unload down my throat again.

You liked that?

No one's done that to me before. I'm hard thinking about it.

So am I.

Where are you?

In bed.

Me too.

Are you touching your cock?

236

No. I'm saving myself for you.

Good boy.

Thank you, sir.

I'm turning the light off now. I'm shattered.

Sleep well.

Goodnight, Oscar.

Goodnight, sir.

For a minute, I lay still, staring at the pixelated letters of our conversation. Still laughing at myself in my head. At how quickly I'd lost my cool and composure.

Almost lost my mind.

But he was worth it. I hadn't met anyone like Tim before. And I couldn't wait to get to know him properly. Learn all about him.

What turned him on and what drove him wild. How hard he could fuck me or how slow and deep and intense he could slide inside. How he liked to cuddle after.

Big spoon always? Sometimes small?

I fantasised about how maybe one day we could become boyfriends and move in together. I could live with him in his place. Help him with his new life. Make a life together.

Away from this disgusting house. Away from my worthless father and the memories of my gutless mother.

Rolling onto my side, I reached over to my bedside table and put my phone on charge. Then I stood up and took off my clothes, dumping them in a crumpled black heap by my feet. Flicking off the light, I climbed back into bed and under my duvet.

'It's going to work,' I whispered to myself in the darkness.

Then, less than a minute later, I fell asleep.

Twenty-seven

I had the same dream that night.

Almost the same.

It began like before. At home in the kitchen with my parents in their wedding outfits. Mum fussing over my black and gold suit, inexplicably back from whatever life she'd chosen over us like she'd never left at all. Dad fit and young and smiling again.

In the blink of an eye, I was outside the same glitching church, its eerie spire twitching and jolting and piercing cloud. Down on the ground, like before, was the same faceless wedding crowd waiting for me. The same woman in black and gold standing by the old wooden doors.

But she looked different: gone was the swirling soup of skin and shadow that had made up her face. Now her features were as clear as day.

She was older than me but young. Late twenties, early thirties. And beautiful. Stunning. She had glossy, shoulder-length blonde hair, high cheek bones and red painted lips pulled straight in neither a smile nor a scowl.

Two dull, sad blue eyes looked at mine, but she wasn't looking at me. She was looking through me, like I was made of glass.

I recognised her. I'd seen her before. Somewhere.

Moving on, I pushed the church doors open and they flung inwards at the slightest touch, crashing against the stone walls inside. Tim turned at the boom, still waiting at the altar in his matching suit.

Black and gold. Emptiness and everything. Beckoning me closer.

I ran. Faster than before but the floor still turned like a treadmill. Pumping my legs as hard as I could, I tried and tried to get closer. But again, it was futile. The ancient, broken tiles fell away, right on cue, and I tumbled into darkness.

The same office materialised around me as I landed in the same green chair. The same computer in front of me. The same nameless folder on the screen. The same video file: Tim and Adam kissing. James in the middle.

All three naked and hungry and hard.

But this time, as the red-haired piggy got spit-roasted raw, his tiny, toned and flawless alabaster body rocking back and forth on his knees and hands between two muscled giants – Adam pumping in and out of his mouth and Tim, my Tim, stretching and filling his hole wider and fuller than I ever had – I wasn't jealous. Or angry.

Or anything I'd felt before.

Instead I laughed. A grin. Then a smirk: no more than a punchy, breathy burst through my nostrils. But once I'd started I couldn't stop. Soon I was howling like a maniac.

I knew what the video meant. What all of it meant. Before I'd been scared. Scared of losing Tim. And jealous. Jealous of Adam's past and James's potential. But now I knew Mr. Price wanted me. He'd told me himself, in his own words. Words I'd read with my own eyes.

Adam and James are nothing next to me.

Standing, I picked up the computer monitor and yanked it away from the desk. Wires strained and snapped

240

but the scene kept playing: their grunts and moans and groans, thrusts and winces louder and closer, looping in my hands.

Raising the screen above my head, I threw it down as hard as I could. Plastic and glass crashed and shattered. Wood splintered and cracked. The monitor exploded in a spray of glistening glass shards, wires and metal. The desk broke in two, clean down the middle.

All around me the sounds of destruction rolled and echoed. But the noises grew louder. Louder and faster; reverberating off the walls and through me like feedback through an amplifier until the booms and bangs became beats and the beats merged together to create an endless, ear-splitting, high-pitched screech.

Then in an instant, as the pitch neared unbearable, silence descended. Heavier and thicker and more oppressive than silent. Like sound had been sucked from the air by an unseen vacuum.

The broken desk vanished. All four walls around me fell backwards and the filing cabinet and chairs and printer disintegrated like sand castles caught in a noiseless gale.

In its place appeared Mr. Price's bedroom. His bed. The same bed I'd just seen in the video but empty; the same bed I'd spent an hour on the evening before. Face down, arse up.

Sitting, I stroked the soft, cotton of his duvet cover. Pulled it to my cheek and breathed in his scent. It smelt mouldy. Then it was ripped out of my hand.

The blonde woman.

She was standing a metre away from me. Hunched over and sobbing soundlessly into the sheet scrunched up in her fists. Her whole body was shaking and convulsing. Her hair hanging forward, hiding her face.

I tried to move. Tried to speak. Couldn't.

She looked up and a blood-curdling shudder rolled through me. Her eyes were completely black, streaming golden tears. Her teeth were bared, but the gold was pouring over her gums and down her chin from cracked lips pulled back in a furious snarl.

Raising a shaking hand, she pointed at my chest.

Then, as sound returned with vigour, air whooshing past my ears like I'd stuck my head out of a car doing a hundred miles an hour, she screamed. Two words. A single syllable each. Both thrust into the void with a sadness and fury and hatred worthy of a lifetime of pain.

'GET OUT!'

I woke with a jolt, panting and wet through with sweat; my hands clutching at my damp bed sheets; my knuckles white and my fingers aching. Letting go, I rubbed my eyes and looked around. I was home. In my room.

Awake.

Letting out a long, deep breath, I stared at the ceiling stain as the unsettling aftermath of my nightmare slowly seeped away with the retreating gloop of unconsciousness.

'It was a dream,' I told myself. 'Just a dream.'

Then I remembered what day it was.

Smiling, I shook my head as fast as my aching neck would allow, and tried to make myself forget the blonde woman's black eyes and tears of molten gold. Swallowed down the all too vivid sorrow and agony of her words.

I have more important things to worry about.

Throwing back my covers like a kid on Christmas morning, I let the air roll over me. My room was cold but

242

the chill soothed my hot, naked flesh. Wiping my forehead with my forearm, I stood up and stretched. Looked down at my cock.

'Good morning.'

Wrapping my fingers around my shaft, I squeezed. Relished the ache through my balls and thighs and calves. My arse cheeks clenching. My hole squeezing tight between them.

'Today's the day,' I said, relaxing out before slowly pulling on myself.

Fast enough to feel good, but slow enough to stay in control of the urges racing through me. Urges telling me to lie down. Spit on my hand. Smear my saliva from base to tip while I thought about him. All the things he'd done to me. All the things he was going to do.

I let go. *Tim Price. Full balls.*

Yawning, I walked to the window and pulled open my curtains. Daylight streamed in, dimmer than any other morning that week.

Too dim.

Flopping onto my bed, I reached over to my bedside table and picked up my phone. Checked the time.

'FUCK!'

Jumping onto my feet and grabbing a towel I raced to the bathroom. Slammed the door shut, locked it and turned on the shower.

'Fuck, fuck, fuck!' I said again, throwing myself under the stream of lukewarm water and furiously brushing my teeth.

It was three in the afternoon. Not only had I slept for fifteen hours I had, at most, forty-five minutes to get ready.

Forty-five measly minutes to shave my arse crack, wash my body from top to toe and shampoo and condition my hair. Forty-five minutes to dry myself, dress myself, dry my hair, do my hair, smash a coffee and get walking.

No time for last-minute press-ups to beef up my pecs and biceps and triceps. No time for a sit-up power session to tighten my abs. No final squats or lunges to ensure my legs and arse were looking their best. All I had was a race against the clock to turn up at Tim's looking barely fuckable.

Thank sweet Jesus I don't need to douche.

Thirty-five minutes later, I was watching the kettle boil in the kitchen, dressed in my go-to outfit: my best, arse-cupping jeans paired with my tightest white t-shirt and burgundy sweater. White jockstrap. Tan suede shoes. My hair had turned out better than expected too. I looked good.

Smart but casual. Smooth and sexy. But I didn't feel smart or smooth or sexy. I felt like shit.

I was tired. That weird, dazed tired you get from too much sleep. But there was something else. A feeling in my stomach, deep down inside my gut. Unsettling and unwanted, wriggling around like a parasite.

Who was she?

I ignored it. It didn't matter. I'd seen a documentary when I was a kid that said humans are visual creatures, and our dreams are made up of what we consciously and subconsciously see around us. She could have been anyone. A woman on the street or on the bus or at school or on TV.

Slamming my empty mug on the counter, caffeine racing through my veins, I grabbed my keys, wallet and coat and made my way to the front door. But as I reached for the door handle it moved downwards and the door came at me.

244

Dad. He was holding a blue plastic carrier bag full of what looked like a six-pack of beer. And he was drunk.

'Look who it is,' he said, stumbling into the hallway.

Collecting himself he leaned against the wall and looked me up and down. I said nothing. No point.

'Aw what's the matter? Don't want to talk to your dear old dad?'

I said nothing.

'Pfft,' he said, pushing himself back to standing; the plastic bag rustling. 'Where you going?'

'Out.'

'Where?'

'Out.'

'On your own?'

'I'm meeting a friend.'

He scoffed.

'You? Who the fuck wants to be your friend?'

Again, I said nothing. His words didn't hurt anymore. They hadn't for a long time.

Plus, going by his choice of vocabulary and level of inebriation, he was only getting started for the day. He was far more interested in getting inside and getting obliterated than getting under my skin.

'Whatever. As if I care,' he said.

Tensing, I passed him slowly. He stank of booze but he let me by without any trouble. He'd never hit me before, but he'd pushed me. Shoved me once or twice.

'For fun'.

Safely outside, I began the fifteen-minute walk to Mr. Price's. It was cold, but the sun was still shining, and its late afternoon rays were strong enough to heat my face and body. It felt nice.

But I still didn't. I couldn't shake the feeling.

With each step, it grew and grew, twisting and turning and squeezing tighter. Flashbacks of the blonde woman strobed my mind as I crossed streets and passed shops and walked along busy roads full of Saturday traffic.

At two-minutes-to-four, I reached Tim's street and by dead on four I was next to his spotless black Audi. Leaning against the cold metal, I closed my eyes and pushed it down one final time.

All the dread and unease and uncertainty and foreboding. All the way down to the place where I kept the things I never wanted to think about again. Like my mother and father and the weak child I once had been.

It was nerves on an empty stomach. My mind playing tricks on me after a bad dream. *Right?*

Wrong.

Twenty-eight

I wish I could say I saw it coming.

That, as my shoes crunched the gravel of Tim's path, the ominous, sickening feeling wriggling around my gut became clear. That, before I crossed the point of no return, I realised what was waiting for me inside, and I turned and ran and cut my losses no matter how much I knew I would lose.

But I didn't. I did exactly what I'd told myself to do.

I swallowed it down. Pushed the dread somewhere so deep and dark I lost it. Replaced it with starry-eyed, teenage fantasies.

Will he kiss me on the doorstep? Or wait until we're away from prying eyes? Will he sweep me off my feet and into his car? Cruise us far away from town to the city somewhere big and shiny and exciting.

Or will he invite me in? Play coy or shy or standoffish to make me want him more? Or will he be all over me? Kiss me, hold me. Tie me up, use me and abuse me. Feed me a shot of his load with a beer chaser.

And what will he be wearing? I'd only ever seen him in his rugby shorts and sports tops. Not that his fashion choices had ever been bad, but I could only imagine how smart and handsome and irresistible he was going to look in a pair of jeans or chinos and a fitted shirt or sweater.

A real man. A gentleman.

As I took the single, moss-speckled stone step up to his front door and lifted my hand, a wave of sickness rolled through me.

It didn't even occur to me, when my knuckles collided against the dark navy, polished wood, pushing the unlocked door open an inch with a low creak, that something might be wrong.

I thought it was a game. A tease. Sir leaving the door open so I, the young, blue-eyed boy could find him waiting inside. Sat ready to bend me over his knee and peal my jeans down. Hungrily pull at my cheeks.

Closing the door gently behind me, I tiptoed through the hallway as quietly as I could. Past the empty living room and the stairway. Past an array of framed photos recently hung, now gently gleaming in the low afternoon light trickling through the frosted-glass window of the front door behind me.

The dining room door was closed but he was in there. I could sense him. Placing my ear against the smooth, cool wood I waited for the initial muffled sounds of contact to smooth away. Then I heard him: the faintest in-and-out of a large, muscled chest rising and falling.

Standing up straight, I stretched out my back. Cracked my neck. Took a deep breath and ran a finger around the waistband of my jockstrap to make sure it wasn't twisted. Decided, that if he was sat on a chair, I would straddle him. Kiss his mouth and neck while I grinded my arse against his crotch and squeezed his muscled flanks between my thighs.

But, if he was standing, I would drop to my knees. Take him in my mouth and down my throat before anything else. I wanted him to know I liked his games.

Finally his star pupil.

Then, I wasn't. I went from nervous and excited to terrified. Desperate for his arms and chest and legs and back and load to weak and unprepared and vulnerable.

To the right, no more than five inches from my eyes, was Tim. Framed in full colour and hidden among a group of ten other smiling faces. A family shot taken on holiday. He was beaming, wide and toothy, and he had his arm around someone. A young blonde woman. *The* young, blonde woman. From my nightmare.

His ex-wife.

I knew I'd seen her before. At school, when she'd dropped Tim off a long time ago. Back when he'd been a teacher. I'd seen her behind the wheel. Beautiful but sad.

Then her haunting scream echoed in my mind.

'GET OUT!'

That was when I knew I needed to leave. I didn't know why but something animal and primal was telling me to turn and run. There was no rational reason, but the squirming sense of foreboding was back from the depths and stabbing furiously inside my gut. Incubated just long enough to burst through my chest.

I'd made a mistake. My quest to claim Tim Price was fundamentally flawed. It had been all along. I'd known it was based on lies and founded on dishonesty, but I hadn't cared. I'd wanted it to work so badly that I'd ignored the truth. Acted like everything would be fine because I'd needed it to be.

Because I need him.

He was going to make my life better. He was going to give it meaning. I'd thought that he could even be the one to convince me that I was going to be ok. That I wouldn't be alone anymore.

But it was too late to run.

'I know you're out there,' he said.

I said nothing. Held my breath and didn't move a muscle.

'Please. I can hear you,' he said.

His voice was calm and void of emotion. Neither friendly nor hostile. An instruction.

Pushing the door open slowly, I slinked through the crack and closed it. Leaning with my back against the door and arms folded, I looked over.

He was sat in the same chair he'd picked the first time I'd been over. Far left corner of the table. On his upper half was a woollen grey jumper, clinging to his body. His legs were open but I could only see his right one – the other obscured by the table top. He was wearing midnight blue jeans.

One of his hands was rested below the table line in his lap and the other gripped a half-full bottle of beer. His posture was slumped and closed off. His shaved head hung slightly; his eyes fixed on the dark green glass in front of him. His feet bare.

'Hey,' I said.

No reply.

Taking a step forward, I ignored the alarm bells ringing in my head and chest and stomach. Cocked my head to the side and coughed. He looked up and saw me for the first time.

For the briefest of moments, he smiled. Kind and genuine. Maybe he liked how well I'd scrubbed up. Or maybe he was just happy to see me. I didn't find out. The look on his face vanished and his eyes turned cold and away.

'You ok?' I said, walking closer.

'Take a seat,' he said, his voice gruff and cracking like he'd been silent all day.

'Ok,' I said, pulling out the chair opposite him and obeying like a submissive puppy.

For ten seconds neither of us spoke. For all ten he didn't look at me. All he did was take a swig from his bottle and place it back slowly and soundlessly.

'Bit early for that?' I said trying to catch his eye.

No use. He simply raised and lowered his eyebrows, his stare on the bottle. Then he spoke.

'We need to talk.'

'Of course,' I said. 'What about?'

There was still a chance. A chance that this had nothing to do with me.

Maybe he'd had a bad day. Bumped into an old friend or colleague. Maybe his past mistakes had come back to haunt him and he needed me. Needed me to hold him and make him feel better and tell him everything was going to be ok.

Wrong again.

'You lied to me,' he said.

My head shook by itself. Five words came out of my mouth on their own accord. My auto-piloted, self-defence mechanism already deployed.

'What are you talking about?' I said.

'Oscar. Stop.'

'Stop what?'

'Stop lying to me.'

'I'm not.'

He scoffed.

'I had a visitor last night,' he said.

'And?'

'And he told me everything.'

'Who?'

Not that I didn't know the answer.

'Adam Stanmore,' he said.

I looked away. To hide the anger spilling across my face. *How could I have been so stupid? How could I have underestimated him?*

I knew he was pathetic enough to try and tear Tim and me apart, but I hadn't expected him to act so soon. I thought I'd had more time.

More time to outsmart that brainless slab of useless muscle.

'Let me guess,' I said.

'No. You don't get to speak.'

'That's not fair.'

'Not fair? You have no right to come into my home and tell me what's fair.'

I said nothing and he took another swig.

'He woke me up in the middle of the night by throwing fucking gravel at my window. I told him to leave but he wouldn't listen. He said he needed to warn me.'

'Warn you? What about?'

'You.'

I said nothing. Shook my head and made a face. A face that asked how he could even consider such an absurd possibility.

It's Adam's word against mine and Adam isn't here.

'That's a bit dramatic, don't you think?' I said.

'Dramatic?' he said. 'He was in tears, Oscar. I've never seen him like that.'

'So? He got the shit kicked out of him by his dad. I doubt things are sunshine and lollipops for him.'

He shook his head. Said, 'You lied to me. You said he's been going around telling people I'm his boyfriend.'

252

'He has!'

'Not according to him. He says you coerced him into telling you where I lived.'

'Why the fuck would I do that?

'So you could find me. Stalk me in the park and throw yourself at me.'

'Bullshit. You know why I did that.'

'You manipulated him. You made him feel like you were on his side and then you tossed him away.'

I laughed. Half at the glorious memory of sticking it to the King of School. The other because I had nothing to worry about.

True though it was, it was hearsay. Unsubstantiated rumour and gossip. It didn't paint me in the best picture, but unlike Adam, I was in the room. And while he may have outsmarted me by a day, I had more acting talent in my little finger than he had in all six feet and six inches of his body.

Standing up and out of my chair, its feet screeching across the floorboards, I put on my finest sneer.

'So, that's it. You're going to listen to him over me? The boy who ruined your marriage and your career?'

He shook his head. Once and then twice. Looked up at me from his chair with pleading eyes.

'Oscar,' he said. 'I don't know who to believe.'

'Believe me!'

'How can I?'

'Why can't you?' I said, sitting back down to his level and making my face warm and caring and friendly. 'You said you wanted me. That you couldn't wait to see me.'

'I couldn't. Honestly, matey, I've been looking forward to seeing you all week. So much so I couldn't believe what he was telling me. I listened to him and then I told him to go.'

'So why the accusations? Why the change of heart?'

'I thought about it. I've *been* thinking about it all day … You did lie to me, Oscar. You pretended you didn't know me.'

'I explained that,' I said, reaching out and stroking his arm.

'I know. But why would he make up something like this?'

'He's having a hard time. You know how it can be.'

Neither of us spoke for almost ten seconds.

'I want to believe you. I really do,' he said.

'You can, Tim, you can. Trust me,' I said, getting out of my seat and sitting in the empty chair next to him.

Placing my hand on his leg, I squeezed his thigh. Reaching out I kissed his neck and cheek. For two seconds, he let me. Then he pulled away and looked at me, his piercing brown eyes almost black.

Searching my soul.

'Prove it,' he said.

'Prove it?'

'Prove to me you're telling the truth.'

I laughed. Said, 'How?'

'Get out your wallet.'

Silence.

'What? Why?'

'Show me your ID.'

'My ID?'

'Yes. Your ID. You told me you're nineteen.'

'I am nineteen.'

'Adam said you're at school together. You're in the same year. You can't be nineteen.'

254

Silence.

'I repeated a year.'

He shook his head like he could smell the lies.

'In my car, when I dropped you home, you looked me in the face and you told me you had no more secrets.'

'I don't. He's lying!'

'So, prove him wrong,' he said. 'Please.'

I said nothing. Like in my nightmare, I couldn't speak.

Twenty-nine

We could have gone around and around in circles.

Trapped in a hopeless loop. Him demanding or begging for the truth. Me pulling more and more lies out of my arse in a desperate attempt to cover my tracks. The dire process repeating and repeating until one of us snaps or storms out or both.

I could have told him I didn't have my wallet on me. Or I didn't have any ID full stop. Saddle up my high horse and get all indignant and offended. It's not a legal requirement to carry any in this country. I could have left it at home. Lost it. Never applied for one in the first place.

But I had applied for it. And I did have it on me. Tucked inside my wallet next to my debit and National Insurance cards. Thin, pink and plastic: my driving license. Good picture. Bad birthdate.

Liar.

He saw it in my face. Otherwise he wouldn't have looked at me like he did. Sad and disappointed. Cold. Then, in a flash, hot and sharp. Searing and angry. Like I'd betrayed him.

Worse than betrayed.

The way his brow crinkled and his top lip snarled, it was like I'd stabbed him in the back. Or slapped his mum on her birthday. Or walked into his house at Christmas and taken a steaming shit on his presents.

The jig was up. He'd caught me out red handed, or in this case, empty handed. No ID. No explanation. But he wasn't saying anything. He just kept staring. Staring and staring like he was seeing me for the first time.

I was no longer the runner from the park who had gone to the school he'd worked at. Now I was an ex-student obsessed.

Gone was the man I'd met in the old creek field: dark and broody and intrigued. And long gone was the man I'd known for the best hours of my life. The muscled power-house that had ruthlessly ploughed me. Stretched my throat and hole open fuller and wider and fulfilled me more than any man.

The sensual, affectionate man smiling at me from the driving seat of his car. Sending me cute text messages. Listening.

That man had gone. And I had no idea how to find him again. No idea what to say.

I'd never been in this position. Sure, I'd lied to plenty of guys in the past. Told them I was a virgin longing to finally have my arse broken in. Or I had a girlfriend but she wouldn't let me fuck her in the back. Something to get them going. Something they could latch onto or lap up to feed their fantasies itching to be acted out with or in or on my toned and eager teenage body.

But I hadn't cared about them. Hadn't cared if they'd found out I was telling porkies. Hadn't cared if it had bothered them. As far as I was concerned they'd been cash machines with cocks. Walking distractions with thick arms, nice abs and nicer cars. I hadn't given two short shits about any of them. Still didn't.

But Mr. Price. He was real. We were real. And sadly, unlike the rest, I couldn't tell him what he wanted to hear. Because he wanted the truth. And the truth was too embarrassing. Too fucked up.

What would I say? That I'd been following him? Watching him run around a park for the last two weeks so I could learn his movements before implementing some master plan to win his heart?

He'll hate me. Or worse, pity me.

'I'm sorry,' I said.

He turned his head away. Looked at the empty beer bottle wedged between his huge hands and sighed. Said nothing.

Reaching out, I touched his forearm. For half a second he allowed it. Allowed me to feel his skin and hair and heat and muscle in a blissful blink. Then he pulled away, still saying nothing.

I tried again. Tried to grab hold. Pull his arm toward me and hold his hand against my cheek. I told myself if he let me I would tell him everything. Explain it all. Tell him why I'd lied. Why I'd used Adam and why he'd deserved it.

Then I would tell him how much I needed him. How he was the first man to ever give me any sense of hope. That maybe, with him by my side, I could have a decent life in this fucked up town. That maybe dreams do come true.

But he shook me off. Pulled his arm away and turned his head so all I could see was his powerful profile and the sublime line of stubble where shaved head met strong neck.

A neck I will never hang off again.

'Please, I'm sorry,' I said.

He shook his head and turned back to face me. Said nothing. Just kept staring at me with unblinking eyes. The muscles in his jaw clenched and throbbing. His body so close but so far away.

'I didn't mean to lie to you,' I said, reaching out for a third time.

Dodging my hand, he grabbed his bottle and stood up.

'Please don't touch me,' he said, looking down at me.

'Please? Tim?'

'No,' he said. 'Don't. You lied to me.'

I said nothing and looked at my hands; the weight of his stare too much for my shoulders.

'Cat got your tongue?' he said.

'I don't know what to say.'

'Admit it.'

'Ok.'

'Ok, what?'

'Ok, yes,' I said, sweat beginning to bead under my hairline; my face red, my palms moist, my skin itching like a colony of fire ants had made me their home. 'I lied to you. I'm not nineteen.'

'How old are you?'

'Eighteen.'

'Prove it.'

'I'm still at school. Adam and I are in the same year.'

'I need proof.'

'Why?'

'I have no idea who you are, Oscar! You could be fifteen for all I know! When I say I can't deal with lies in my life, I mean it!'

'Ok, ok,' I said, reaching around my back and pulling my wallet out of my back pocket, his voice still booming in my ears.

Opening the tattered leather, I took out my ID. Handed it to him over the table. He put his beer down and looked at the rectangle of laminated plastic for exactly three seconds before giving it back.

'Thank you,' he said.

'You're welcome,' I muttered.

'Now get out.'

'What? Why?'

'Why do you think?'

'I'm still legal! I haven't done anything wrong!'

'Haven't done anything wrong?' he said, placing his hands on the dining table and leaning towards me; his biceps and triceps and pecs bulging under the thin grey cotton of his jumper.

'You told me you were nineteen,' he said.

'So what?' I said, still sweating under his scrutiny. 'People lie about their age all the time.'

'Yeah. You're not wrong. People do. And you know what? I wouldn't have cared. I wouldn't have given a flying fuck if it'd been as simple as you adding a few months on because you didn't want to put me off.'

'Then why? Why should I leave? Why do you hate me now?'

Closing his eyes, he took a deep breath. A short, sharp hiss filling the room as he inhaled. I felt his outbreath, warm and moist and smelling of beer.

Opening his eyes his face was softer. But still an eternity from the face I'd been in awe of, lying in his arms.

'I don't hate you, Oscar,' he said.

'Yes, you do,' I said, my voice weak and pathetic.

'No, I don't. But I don't get you.'

I looked up and the room was suddenly blurry. There were tears in my eyes. Wiping them in my elbow crease I shook myself out of it.

Don't fucking cry.

Taking a deep breath of my own, I focused. Controlled my emotions. Pushed the sadness and pain down and away.

'If you don't hate me,' I said, as calm and collected as I could. 'Why do you want me to leave?'

'Because of Adam.'

I said nothing. Shook my head and made a face that said I couldn't believe he was still taking that over-sized moron's side.

Bad idea. Mr. Price's fire did not need any more fuel.

'Stop it!'

'He's lying!' I said.

'Why?'

I said nothing.

'Why would he make up something like that? Why would he beg to talk to me? Tell me through streaming eyes that you'd sat on his cock and let him fuck you for information.'

'I don't know!' I tried to say but ended up shouting. 'He's fucked up.'

'He's fucked up? That's rich.'

'Excuse me?'

'You stalked me! You literally threw yourself at me!'

'I told you why I did that.'

'How can I believe anything you've told me?'

I said nothing. My mind was blank. All I could focus on was the sinking feeling in my stomach. My guts twisting and knotting and tightening. Nausea rolling through me like polluted waves.

'Exactly,' he said, shaking his head at my silence. 'I can't believe you. I gave you a chance, Oscar. To tell me the truth. You looked me in the eye and lied to my face. I don't want anything to do with you.'

'Please, Tim,' I said, words finally working. 'Don't do this. I need you.'

'Need me? *You* need *me*?'

I nodded fast. Tried to think of what to say. How to phrase it so he would listen. But he didn't give me a chance.

'You don't need me. You used me. Which, hey, I really shouldn't be complaining about should I? A boy like you, who gets anyone he wants, no matter the cost. I should be grateful. Thankful you even bothered to look at me.'

'That's not true.'

'Whatever, Oscar. The truth is I can't see you anymore. I can't keep second-guessing my life and the people in it. I lived a lie for too long.'

'But I only said those things so I could be with you. I didn't want to hurt you.'

Shaking his head, he walked out of the room to the kitchen. Bare feet clapped against tiles and the fridge opened. A bottle of beer hissed. Just one. Then came the slow, morbid applause of naked soles again.

He appeared by the doorway with his fresh beer in his hand. Leant against the frame and took a swig.

'Ok. You didn't want to hurt me. I suppose I can see that. But you knew. You knew all along. About my ex-wife and my history. About Adam. And you sat right there.

262

Right there, in my dining room, listening to me tell you a story you already knew just so you could what? Build my trust? Manipulate me?'

My mouth opened but nothing came out.

'What kind of person does that?' he said.

Silence descended again. My chest numb.

'Answer me!'

Thirty

I should have told him the truth.

That I loved him.

Explained to Tim, the first man to make my heart soar inside my chest like a lone bird in the dead of night, that there was no wonder he didn't "get me".

I should have told him that the kind of person who does the kind of things I'd done isn't reasonable. Or understandable. Or normal. I should have told him that I was fucked-up, poisoned and lost.

I should have explained, begged him to forgive me, that since my mum had left and my dad had rotted away with loneliness, I didn't know how to be good or kind or honest. I didn't know how to love. How to express it or feel it.

And worst of all, I didn't know how to recognise it. Love wasn't on my radar.

Now I know love. I see it and feel it. And, most importantly, understand why I hadn't. Why at eighteen I was unwilling to accept how afraid and alone I was because I'd been abandoned. Tossed aside and forgotten by the people who had supposed to have loved me the most.

They had, for a while. I'd tasted a good life. A normal life. But then they'd left and my world hadn't just flipped, it had flipped, fissured and imploded until only miniscule chunks of ripped apart memories were left, spinning and spiralling in the gaping, icy void left inside my head and heart.

My mother gone without a goodbye. My father distorted beyond recognition. My parents snuffing out the embers of happiness in cruel, cold, selfish instants.

Everybody leaves.

But that's the so-called beauty of hindsight, isn't it? Only knowing which path to walk thanks to the clarity of the future. It all seems so clear looking to the past. So easy and obvious away from the storm of confusion raging and thrashing around the present.

I should have told him. Told him everything. But I didn't. Because I didn't know any better.

Want to know a sad secret? Truth is, I learned the importance and power of honesty four years and many miles away from that fateful afternoon at Mr. Price's, dumbstruck and destroyed and unable to convince him to keep me.

Tim was just the beginning. The beginning of my descent into depravity.

'I'm waiting for your answer,' he said, still standing over me; still staring me down; still furious.

I wanted to speak. Say something. Anything. But I was still lost for words. Still stuck between gutted and horrified. Powerless to make an excuse or lie quick enough. Unable to find a solution to make everything go back to how it was.

Back to the two of us.

Just him and me, in his car and out of town. Far away from his ex-wife and my nightmares. Far away from my stupid lies. Far away from everything.

'All I can say is I'm sorry,' I said, accepting the truth that there was no way out.

No dishonesty big enough or clever enough.

'That's all you've got?' he said.

'Please, Tim. It won't happen again. I promise.'

'It won't happen again?'

'Never.'

'You don't get it, do you?' he said.

'I do!'

'No, you don't! You're like a child in the classroom. Apologising for the sake of it. Saying you won't do it again because that's what you think you're meant to say. But you don't even know what you did or why it hurts, do you?'

'I do, I do. I lied to you.'

'And?'

And? And what?

'I don't know,' I said.

'You see, Oscar. This is what I'm talking about. You knew my story. You knew my wife left me because of Adam. You *must* have known, or at least realised how confusing and fucked up a situation that was for me. But you used it.'

'No I didn't.'

'Yes, you did.'

'How?'

Shaking his head, he took another swig of beer. But this time he slammed the bottle down on the dining table. Glass collided against wood and made me jump. Amber liquid fizzed white and foamed down the bottle neck and over his knuckles.

He didn't even move. Didn't flinch. Didn't look down. Just let the beer run over him and onto the table as his empty eyes punctured through me.

Seeing me for exactly what and who I am.

266

'You think I wanted to tell you that story?' he said, barely able to control the fury in his voice. 'You think I wanted to remember? Dredge up the past? Parade my skeletons for your amusement?'

'No,' I muttered.

'So what do you think I would have wanted?'

'I don't know,' I said again, looking at my hands, locked tight together in my lap.

For a moment, there was silence. I looked up into his eyes and he looked away. Then, letting out a deep breath through his mouth, his thick lips pursing, he hung his shaved head and rubbed his crown.

Fingernails gently scratched against stubble. Once, twice, three times. Then wooden chair legs screeched against floorboards as he took a seat.

'I would have liked to have the chance to be me, without being the guy who cheated on his wife with a schoolboy. I would have liked to meet a cute guy and start a future together, or at least something real. The last thing I wanted was to bring up my sordid past.'

I said nothing, even though I still wanted to speak. Tell him we could have a future together; that I could be that guy.

But I'm not that guy.

'You used me,' he said.

I still said nothing. Just shuffled in my chair as the painful realisation hit. My cheeks burning red as my options became black and white. My palms damp. My future barren.

'And then, you lied about it. Over and over. Even when I gave you a chance to come clean … I'm sorry but no. No more. No more you or Adam or any of this. Please, Oscar, just get out.'

His anger was gone and in its place was sadness. I knew it well. It was the sadness of loneliness; the grief of having no one.

But I couldn't empathise. Not properly. Empathy needs love, like a car needs fuel, and there had been just enough left inside of me to spark my reaction. But that was it, a spark. Running on fumes.

I had no choice but to do what I did best. Take his pain and my mistakes, his anger and my lies, everything that had gone so wrong and swallow it. Force it down deep to where the love should have been and lock it away.

Tim and I were over and whatever hope he'd had for me was dead. There would be nothing more. Nothing more than memories.

The crunch of his trainers against gravel. His inquisitive eyes. His rough but gentle hands massaging my thigh. The sound of his tread through the dark forest. The snap of twigs and the crunch of leaves. The rich smell of wet earth.

His lips against mine. His huge hands running through my hair. His trainer laces digging into my wrists. His cock stretching my jaw and slamming into the back of my throat. His deep grunts and manly groans. His hot, salty load streaming into my stomach.

Following him home. Walking into his house. The refreshing tingle of cold beer against my friction-burnt throat. His fingers playing with my tongue and mouth. Feeling them slide between my other cheeks and inside my hole.

The sting, the burn and the rush. The rush of dreams becoming vivid reality.

The soft fibres of his carpet under my bare feet. Then stomach. His tongue against my hole. The heat. The wetness.

His bedroom. The cloudlike plushness of his bedsheets. The power of his body on mine. The eye-rolling intensity of him forcing his way inside me. Joining us together for what seemed like an eternity and no time at all.

A spark in the darkness.

Then I extinguished him. I stood and turned and left his dining room without looking back. I didn't want to remember him like this. I didn't want to mourn.

Everything after that was a blur.

All I remembered was getting home and raiding Dad's alcohol stash. Drinking myself stupid and smoking joint after joint in my bedroom as he snored in the room next door. Then waking hungover and tired but repeating until I passed out again.

The weekend over, school rolled around. I thought about ditching but they would call the house. So I forced myself to go in. Forced myself to focus on the lessons and keep my mind busy.

I was in my last year. *The same year as Adam.* A-levels and university on the horizon. And university meant escape.

Three days of endless school later, gossip started circulating about Adam. That him and that "little ginger gay boy" were dating. Gossip confirmed an hour later via two texts. One from each.

That afternoon I skipped my lessons to walk the route I'd been avoiding. Down Overslade Lane and through the mundane part of town. To Tim's.

His house was empty. A sold sign out front.

No.

I came close to breaking that day. Closer than ever to letting the pain I'd been holding out. Surrendering to the agony in my heart and the darkness in my mind. Doing something irreversible. Something I wouldn't be able to regret.

Do it.

But I didn't.

Later at home, I changed my mind. Something happened. Something amazing. Something I would never have seen coming in a million years.

I got an email while I was writing a note. It was from the gay supplies store in the city I'd bought lubricant from. An advert. Spam advertising that had popped up on my computer screen about a new app for the iPhone.

A dating app that would show me how far away the nearest guy was. Tell me how to get to them through its GPS system. A faceless orange mask with empty eyes and untold promises. And it was free.

If I have an iPhone.

The next day I didn't go to school. I took my dad's credit card from his wallet and took a trip into town instead. A few hours later, sat in my room and watching my new phone load into life, I realised I had more to live for.

Gone were the days wasting hours pretending to care about the boys on MSN. No more would I care about the men on Gaydar taking hours or days or even weeks to reply. Even the pain of Adam and James and Mr. Price was suddenly dulled by the growing excitement inside my stomach and groin, and the game-changing realisation in my head.

A multitude of thumbnails, tiny squares of skin and muscles and smiles, shone from the screen in my hands. Radiating possibilities.

As far as I was concerned, life was just beginning.

To be continued …

About Jack Ladd

Jack Ladd was born in the UK, grew up in a small English town and fled to Sydney, Australia, as soon as he could. There he spent many years discovering the world, the people who call it home, and, most importantly, himself. Oscar and his adventures are based on true events.

Other Books by the Author

The Oscar Series
Oscar Bachelor of Arts (available online or coming soon to retailers)

The Down Under Series
Oscar Down Under: Part One

Connect with Jack Ladd

Thank you for reading. If you would like to learn more, or stay up to date with Ladd's current online tale, *Oscar Bachelor of Arts*, follow the links below:

Facebook: https://www.facebook.com/jackladdODU/
Instagram: @jackladd_odu
Website: www.jackladd.org